Pleiades Rising

Scott Gesinger

For Melissa. I would choose you in any life I could ever live.

For Dad, thank you for all the wonderful books and for all your encouragement.

Author's Note:

The collection of stories contained here was written over the course of a few months in the small loft of my townhome outside of St. Paul, Minnesota. I had finished my first novel, and was tired of writing query letters to agencies and publishers that quite possibly never looked past the subject line of their emails. I needed to get back in the saddle and ride the writing horse again. My wife, Melissa, suggested that I take a few of the ideas I had for stories and see if they would work in short form. It was a great suggestion. The frustration of drafting query letters to people that I knew would often times never read them fell away, and I could dive deep into my own little worlds again. My wish for these stories is that they will intrigue you, frighten you, and most of all, make you think about life, the universe, and everything.

"The Nightfield Murders" was inspired by a painting titled "Krahe" by Rudi Hurzlmeier. I saw it a few years ago when Melissa and I were on our honeymoon on Vancouver Island (a.k.a. heaven). I was intrigued by the simple scene of a crow, his feathers pulled around him like a black overcoat, walking through a winter's field. He wears shoddy black boots and is chewing on a dried stem of hay. It is beautiful and lonely. I would look at the painting, then gaze out of my window into the corn field across the road, watching the crows gather there. The story that was born out of this is one that I found extremely fun to write, and it always puts me in a whimsical mood to think of the adventures that Krahe and Corbeau will have as time goes by. If you love them as much as I do, be happy—they will return in future stories.

"Jenny on the Milk Carton" takes a more serious turn. When I was a kid, a boy about my age was abducted not too far from where I lived. His name was Jacob Wetterling, and I can recall to this day the sorrowful, pleading face of his mother on the news. Ever since Jacob was abducted by a strange man as he rode his bike with his brother and a friend that day, his brave mother has not let anyone forget that he is still missing. I read a story in the newspaper about a man who looked like one of the age-progressed photos of Jacob, and how he had to keep convincing people he was not the missing soul. It kept me awake, and one by one, the pieces for this story fell into place. I mean for the story to be, in the end, one of great hope. I often wonder what has happened to Jacob, and even though I know the end result was probably tragic, I'd like to think that he's happily unaware of who he was, living a good life somewhere right now.

I wrote "The Revelation of Pastor Henry" after becoming completely fed up with watching people who claim to be Christians doing the exact opposite of what I feel are the ideals of Jesus. As Gandhi said, "I like your Christ. I do not like your Christians. They are so unlike your Christ." Take off your WWJD bracelet, stop listening to manipulative politicians who say God would vote for them, and just be kind to someone who needs it. It doesn't take a church, it doesn't take a preacher, it only takes your heart.

I base many of the things I write on dreams. "The Good Life" is one of these stories. The story follows, for the most part, the dream. I think that most of us wonder how life could have been different if we had done one little thing, like caught the interception while scouts watched the game, or asked out the pretty girl who seemed too shy to come over and say hi. In the end, the life each of us lives can only be as good as we live it.

The idea for "Sirens' Fade" came to me one night as Melissa and I were in a tiny bar taking a winter break in Arkansas. I saw one of those old fallout shelter signs on the wall, and began examining the people around us as they danced, drank, and laughed. What would we all do if we were not in the small brick basement space to have a good time, but to escape a certain and horrible fate? In this story, I decided to focus on people in three different places. Some of them are related to each other, but exactly how is up to your interpretation. Our world has come to the brink of an accidental nuclear war several times, and the threat of annihilation did not die with the Cold War.

"Father McKenzie's Kitchen" is my favorite story of this bunch. It is, to me, a classic horror tale, and is my homage to the wonderful short story collections and novels by Stephen King that kept me awake at night, not sure if I wanted to read more or to hide under the covers. One of the most frightening experiences of my life was when, in the middle of reading "Pet Sematary" one night in bed, the head of my mattress fell through the frame and onto the floor. I have no idea why it fell, but I don't think any other teenage boy ever screamed so loud for his dad to come and rescue him.

Finally, there is "Zulu Operator." In the process of writing these stories, I have a few people read a first draft to give me a feel for how a reader will react to a story, then I have those same folks read the final draft to proof it for spelling, punctuation, etc. Everyone who read this collection as I put it together fell in love with this story. It was inspired mainly by two songs that I think have a great spy feel to them, "Strong Black Vine" by Tori Amos, and "Holdin' on to Black Metal" by My Morning Jacket. I would play the songs over and over, and try to picture what a good spy story would look and feel like. As I wrote it, I wasn't sure if it would have enough action, suspense, and thrills, but in the end I think that it delivered. Like the characters in "The Nightfield Murders" you can expect to see some of the players from "Zulu Operator" again in other stories.

Finally, I just want to say thank you. Without a reader, these stories are only words on paper. I hope you enjoy them, and I hope that they can become your friends as much as they have become mine.

SG

Contents

The Nightfield Murders

Krahe cruised above the houses of the village that bordered Nightfield at about a hundred feet. The crow liked this altitude because it was high enough to avoid detection by most humans or domesticated animals below, but low enough that he could still see what was happening on the ground quite well, and an occasional insect would wander by that he could gobble up as he flew.

He could see Nightfield coming up now, beautiful in the spring sun with the first green shoots of corn poking up from the broken ground. He descended to about sixty feet, then looked around for who had made the emergency call. He saw six crows in a circle around what looked to be a dead adult male crow. Krahe made slow, large circles as he descended to the ground, taking in the entire scene around the small group below.

He floated to a gentle landing near the circle of crows, and walked over to them quietly. Near his landing point, there was a small shoot of dry hay which he picked up and stuck in his mouth to chew on. It seemed that chewing a stick of some dry item or other always helped Krahe think. The circle saw him coming, and slowly parted to let him in. A young crow spoke up.

"Detective Krahe, very nice to meet you, sir." He stepped forward and bowed. Krahe silently returned the bow. "My name is Corbeau."

"Very nice to meet you, Corbeau," Krahe said. "I came as soon as I heard the call. I was feeding on Turkey Hill, so it must have been relayed at least twice."

"Well, you still made it quickly."

Another crow, fat and snobbish, spoke up. "I don't see what we need a detective here for, boys. This was obviously an attack by a cat. A murder, but not by one of our kind."

Another of the circle piped up and said, "Visto, you know as well as us that death by cat is not murder, it's simply nature. We've had enough of your New Age nonsense."

Visto replied, "These blasted cats! You'll stand by while they kill every last one of us, won't you?"

Corbeau turned to the group of crows. "It is always best to be on the safe side, so for now we should look into this as we would any other suspicious death. Now, gentlemen, if you don't mind, I believe that Krahe and I should investigate this death in private."

The other five crows that had been in the circle murmured to each other a little bit and slowly began putting space between themselves and the body, but none took wing. Krahe looked at the body, then said loudly to Corbeau, "This your first case, Corbeau?" The younger crow nodded. "Yes, well, memorize the faces around you. Anyone who has this much interest in something as gruesome as our investigation must obviously be considered a suspect."

With that, the fat crow named Visto chimed in to say, "Come on, boys. There's a jousting tournament down at the river bank. Wouldn't want to miss that, eh?" The five took wing, and in a few moments were gone.

Corbeau smiled at Krahe. "Thanks. I was wondering if they'd ever get out of here."

Krahe nodded. "You're new on the job?"

"Two weeks. I've barely been out of academy."

"Did you train under Longbill?"

"I did, yes."

Krahe grunted approval, then turned to the body. The dead crow lay on the dirt between two rows of fresh corn stems. As Krahe observed and took notes, he asked Corbeau "What have you noted so far, old man?" His voice was deep, and very proper. It commanded respect, and others would follow the instructions of that voice almost without thought.

Corbeau quietly cleared his throat and tried to pay attention to how much his voice could command respect. "I saw that it looks as if he was alive when he hit the ground. See those scratches in the dirt there? Looks like he struggled around a bit."

"Yes, yes. Very good. Did you see these bites?"

"I did. Obviously a cat. I did some checking, and there is only one cat in the local clowder that is known to kill prey and leave without eating the victim."

2

Krahe asked, "Does he kill for sport all the time, or eat his kill now and then?"

Corbeau replied, "He'll eat it sometimes."

"Good work. We'll have to check into that cat a little later."

"I also noticed his eyes, Krahe. Quite bizarre behavior, even for a cat that kills for sport."

The dead bird's face was turned away from Krahe. He walked to the other side of the body and looked. Both eyes were gone. Krahe made a "Hmmmmm" sound. He turned to Corbeau, and said, "There's at least one more thing to note about this body."

Corbeau shrugged. "I didn't see anything else to note, Krahe." It didn't surprise Corbeau that Krahe would find something he missed. The detective was nearly fifteen years old, and had been well known for his investigation skills since he was ten. It was no disgrace to miss something that only Krahe would notice.

"Do you have many members of your flock with purple wingtips?"

"Purple? I don't think I've ever noticed a purple wingtip at all, Krahe."

Krahe pointed to the outstretched, broken right wing of the deceased. "Look here. The last few feathers."

"Well, I'll be. You've got to see it from just the right angle, but when you do, that purple really jumps out, doesn't it?"

"It certainly does."

"What could that possibly have to do with whether or not he was murdered?" Corbeau asked.

"I don't know. I do think, however, that murder is indeed what we are investigating, old man. What is the name of that cat?"

"I thought you said this was murder. Cats, well, that's just natural. Like a disease, or being hit on the roadway while eating carrion."

"Death by cat is natural, yes," Krahe replied. "I'm not one of those new-age crows who believes that we should hold cats, humans, foxes, and other predators accountable for their natural behaviors."

"Thank goodness for that!"

3

"However, I do want to find out what that cat knows. What do you know about him?"

Corbeau said, "He calls himself Tiger—"

"*Every* cat calls himself Tiger."

"Right. His domesticated name is Cottonball. He's dark gray stripes with a white belly, a gray tail and deep green eyes. He usually is let out of his house around dusk and hunts the field until around ten, when he returns home for the rest of the evening."

"And what time is he let out in the morning?"

"Around eight, returning home again about four in the afternoon. But during daylight hours, he rarely is in the field."

"Okay. So he did his work on this old chap—oh, by the way, what is this crow's name, Corbeau?"

"Hawkins. If you don't mind me saying, Krahe, it took you some time to ask."

"Names don't mean much when you're dead on the ground, Corbeau. Who names their child after one of our predators?"

"He comes from a notoriously rough family. Two brothers, Eagle and Gust. His parents run the jousting club."

"We'll look into that later."

"Do you think it could be unsanctioned jousting gone too far, Krahe?"

"I don't think so, no."

"It almost looks like he landed with that wing outstretched. That certainly would have broken it."

"Yes. Especially if there was another crow on top of him as he fell. Another crow that landed on him, pecked out his eyes, and either left him to die or who has a four-legged friend who could finish the job during his nightly patrol of the field."

Krahe and Corbeau flew together to the jousting matches that had been organized at the river bank. Krahe was sure that by now Hawkins' family would have heard about his murder. He wondered how it might affect the tournament.

As they flew close to the jousting match, Krahe could see a small flock on a tree below him and Corbeau. Visto, the crow who had blamed a cat for Hawkins' death, was shouting to the others

4

about wanting to kill a cat in revenge. Krahe pointed down to him and said, "Quite the angry fellow." Corbeau nodded in reply.

They could see an epic joust ahead of them as they approached the wide, blue Mississippi below. Two crows twirled and pecked at each other in the air. Finally, one of them got the better of the other, and the defeated crow, a few black feathers floating to earth beneath him, retreated to the trees on the bank. The watching flock issued a mix of cheers and boos from the trees. Seeds and whittled sticks were exchanged as payment for the many illegal bets that had been placed.

Krahe and Corbeau landed in the middle of the ruckus. A young female on the same branch as the two approached Corbeau. She said to him, "Next joust is Gust versus Wormwood. Three-to-one odds on Gust. After that is an open slot against Eagle. Eight-to-one odds on Eagle against any opponent." Krahe hopped to another branch.

Corbeau turned to her and said, "Madam, I am an officer of the law."

She looked startled. "Oh, my. You won't..."

"Arrest you? Of course not. As far as I'm concerned betting ought to be as legal as flying; it's just as natural for us crows. But since it is not legal, I must not take part in it. The joust, for me, is simply entertainment."

"Oh. In that case, maybe I can just share your branch?"

"Of course." Corbeau bowed, then turned back to the action in the sky. Gust had just taken wing. He was a huge crow, his iridescent feathers almost gleaming black. Krahe hopped over from the branch he had wandered over to with a new chewing twig in his beak. "Corbeau, look at his wing tips. That purple color must be a family trait."

Corbeau replied, "Do you think the killer mistook one brother for the other?"

"It certainly is possible. Who's your friend?" Krahe motioned to the female.

"I don't know." Corbeau turned to her and smiled, "Dear, your name?"

"Lenore. Pleased to meet you both, Corbeau and, uh..."

Krahe politely smiled. "Krahe." They bowed to each other, then turned to watch the next joust. Wormwood had just taken flight, climbing to an altitude above Gust. As he waited for the match to start, Gust yelled out to the crowd, "This fight is for my dear brother, Hawkins! May he rest in peace!"

The crows cawed out their approval. Gust pumped his wings hard to gain altitude, and as he climbed, Wormwood dropped straight down. They passed close by each other, Gust climbing swiftly and Wormwood dropping at a frightening rate. The crowd cheered in approval. Now, with their positions changed, Gust began a slow circling descent toward Wormwood. As Wormwood turned and began to take a high angle of attack to gain altitude, Gust dropped and smacked him hard on the tail feathers, knocking a few of them out. Wormwood squawked in pain and tried a mid-air turn to pursue Gust. Before he could even get all the way around, Gust had swung into a fast upward glide, and rammed Wormwood's right wing. Wormwood twirled in the air for a second, hanging in the sky then falling. The crowd gasped.

Wormwood flapped and adjusted himself out of the spin, then decided he had had enough and retreated to the trees. Gust flew a victory lap around the banks of the river, then landed near the water to rest and take a drink. Krahe pointed to a tree on the other side of the banks. "That must be his parents."

Corbeau nodded. "Indeed. Do they look especially sad to you, Krahe?"

"Not in the least. How about to you, Lenore?"

"Well, every time one of their sons wins a joust, they make out like kings," she said. "I've heard they have an extra nest just for winnings. Not that it matters, but it tells you something about them that they still held the joust today. I guess a dead offspring, while sad, is almost expected at some point, no matter who your family is or how wealthy. We *are* wild animals, after all." With that final statement, she leaned in toward Corbeau and winked. He uncontrollably smiled at her.

Krahe noticed that the crowd had quieted down some. "Corbeau, old man, why don't we fly over to the parents after the matches, and ask them a few questions?"

Corbeau nodded. "Of course. It looks like the jousting might be over now." With that, he took wing. Lenore and Krahe both shouted, "Corbeau, no!"

The crow running the joust, Gust's father, spoke to the crowd. "Exciting! Our next contestant has taken wing to challenge Eagle!"

Corbeau looked around nervously and said to himself, "Oh, my. I should have waited, it seems."

Lenore turned to Krahe. "What do we do?"

Krahe sighed. "He's just graduated academy. I suppose all we can do is hope they're still teaching the lads to fight nowadays."

The black bird that took wing next looked to Krahe almost impossibly large for a crow. Lenore pointed to the beastly thing, and said, "That's Eagle."

Krahe chuckled, and said, "Well named. I think I'm going to place a bet or two."

Corbeau saw Eagle climbing in altitude from below. His first thought was that the brothers probably practiced together. He began climbing in altitude ahead of the other crow, going over the strategy he had just seen Gust use. He flapped and raced higher, but soon enough, he could hear the beating of wings of the faster bird behind him.

Corbeau cupped his wings and tail as a sort of air break, and Eagle swept past him, unprepared for any contact. Corbeau now cupped his wings to slowly descend for a second, then tucked them to his body and allowed himself to fall rather than actually diving.

Corbeau looked back, and saw Eagle diving hard behind him. Corbeau untucked his wings and darted to the left. Eagle tried to turn to stay over his target, but missed, too large to make such a tight maneuver. As he passed Corbeau, Eagle tried putting on the brakes, but Corbeau had circled and was now diving right behind him.

Corbeau hit Eagle's back with a *thud*, hammering the back of the larger crow with his beak as they fell toward the water. They were only about ten feet from the surface before Eagle was able to break and gain altitude again. Corbeau, not having had his back just pecked badly, could climb faster, and he stayed right on Eagle's tail, pecking at him over and over until finally the large beast of a bird shouted "*Enough!*"

Corbeau immediately broke off his attack and flew to the place where Eagle's parents watched the matches. He looked across the river to Krahe and Lenore, saw Krahe nod approvingly, and decided that it would be best to meet up after the matches. Corbeau turned to the old crow running the joust. "Excuse me, Mister, uh…"

"Nimble. My name is Nimble. That's my son you just embarrassed out there."

"Yes. I would apologize, except—"

"Except that beating your opponent is the point of the joust," Nimble said with a sly grin. "No apologies in this game, lad. Your winnings are in the tree over there by the big rock. The young crow there will pay you."

"I wanted to ask you a question or two if I could, sir."

"I'm a busy crow."

"Yes, yes, I know. I'm investigating the death of Hawkins. I'm sorry to bring it up here."

Nimble grimaced and narrowed his eyes at Corbeau. "And do you think that starting the conversation with a joust against one of his grieving brothers is appropriate? What are they teaching young crows these days about manners? I think I might like to see your supervisor."

Corbeau had no supervisor. That wasn't how things worked with crows. To have a real job, to do something other than spend your time hunting, jousting, mating, and sleeping, was a choice to a bird. He could not be fired, or reprimanded. Corbeau, wanting to appease Nimble, pointed across the river to Krahe. "He's there, sir."

"He doesn't look like any crow from the Council of Intelligence." The Council was the loosely organized governing body of the flock.

Corbeau replied, "Oh, he's not on the Council, sir. Just a detective like myself."

8

Nimble nodded and gave a "*Hmph!*" He watched silently as the next joust began, and then addressed Corbeau again. "Well, get on with it. What do you want to know?"

"Was there anyone who may have wanted to hurt Hawkins?"

"No. He had few real rivals in the joust; never was much of a competitor and lost more than he won. He was best for practice but not much more."

"Any reason why anyone might have had it out for him?"

Nimble narrowed his eyes at Corbeau again. "What are you getting at?"

"Nothing, sir. I just wanted to rule out any possibility that another crow may have had anything to do with his death."

"I heard it was a cat. Perfectly natural. A noble way to die, in fact; as long as you injure the damned beast."

"When was the last time you saw Hawkins?"

"Oh, it was probably about six last night. He was off to meet some friends. I suppose they were going to hang around until dark and do some night hunting. Always a foolish thing, night hunting. Look now, there's Eagle. If you don't mind, I'd like to end the matches for the day soon, and spend a little time with my two surviving sons. I'd clear out if I were you; Eagle's never been beaten before today, and he looks none too happy about his first time."

"Yes, sir. Thank you." Corbeau turned, but before taking flight, he stopped and faced Nimble again. "Just one more thing, sir, if I could. Those purple feathers on your wing tips—"

"Oh, these?" Nimble held out his wing tip and looked to the purple feathers on it. "Ha! Family trait on my mother's side that got passed down. You can always tell one of my bloodline!" With that he hopped off to meet Eagle, who did indeed look ready to boil steam from his ears. The crowd cheered as the final match finished.

Corbeau took off for the tree that Nimble had pointed out to him, curious to see what he had won. When he got there, a juvenile male crow smiled, chuckled, and said, "Well, my man! Looks like you got the best of Eagle! Nobody's done that before.

I've got something good for you." The crow turned and dug around in a hole where the trunk split off in two directions. He came up with a fresh minnow and a bulbous green grub.

Corbeau smiled. "Thank you! Those look delicious!" He took the rewards and flew across the river (safe to do now that the matches were over) and landed on the branch where Krahe and Lenore waited. He set the meal down in the middle of them.

"For my new friends," he said, smiling.

Krahe and Lenore chuckled. Lenore said, "That's it, then?"

Corbeau, offended at her lack of enthusiasm, said firmly but politely, "What do you mean by that? This is a good meal for three crows!"

Krahe, smiling, said to Corbeau. "Good man, we both placed large bets on you. We've got enough winnings to feed the three of us for a week. Maybe longer."

Corbeau's beak dropped open. "Krahe! You placed a bet? But... but..."

"Illegal," he said with a wink. "Yes, I know. And I don't care." Lenore laughed at Krahe's statement and Corbeau's look of shock.

Corbeau turned to her. "You, I expect this from. And I've only known you a half hour. But you," he turned back to Krahe, "You are a crow of the law. Sworn to uphold it!"

"Corbeau, my good friend, one thing you must understand about me. I do this job for the pleasure of solving the puzzles of blood and deceit. I'm no more a saint than you are a fish."

Corbeau slumped his shoulders, and quietly ate with Krahe and Lenore, disappointed that on his first murder case, he found his hero to be nothing more than a thrill seeker. As he ate, he noticed Lenore moving closer and closer to him. Twice, their beaks touched lightly while they nibbled at the minnow.

When the meal was finished, the sun was low in the west. Lenore turned to Corbeau, and asked, "May I see you again sometime, Corbeau? You were brilliant in the joust. Maybe we can meet for breakfast?"

Corbeau straightened his posture, unconsciously smiled, and said, "I would be delighted, my lady." He bowed low to her. She giggled, kissed his cheek, and flew off.

Krahe raised an eyebrow. "You'd better ask her where and when, old man."

"Oh my! Yes!" Corbeau flew after her. Krahe watched as they formed a single silhouette for a few seconds, then broke apart. Corbeau landed on the branch again, smiled and said, "You, I'll meet for lunch, Krahe."

"That sounds splendid. But we have more work to do tonight. I want to meet that cat."

***

It was a bit past sunset as Krahe and Corbeau waited in a tall oak tree that stood on the edge of Nightfield. Krahe pointed to the north, where the humans' houses stood. "There he is, Corbeau."

Corbeau looked and saw a shape slinking away from the houses. In the dark it didn't really look gray, but more of a lighter shade of darkness as it crossed the street into Nightfield. They took off and circled high above, well out of sight range of the cat.

The feline slinked through the low green shoots in the field for a while, then stopped. They watched as its back legs wound up, and it pounced on a small field mouse. While the cat was busy chomping the tiny thing, the two crows landed in front of it, about ten feet away from the cat and six or seven feet away from each other.

The cat looked up from its snack, licked some blood off its lips, and asked, "Who are you two, another couple of New Age hippies who want to tell me how wicked I am for eating birds? And why are you spaced apart like that? You make me nervous."

Krahe spoke. "You're a cat. Everything makes you nervous. We're spaced like this so that if you try to attack one of us, the other can attack you in return."

The cat flexed his paws so that his claws poked out. He growled. "What do you want?"

Corbeau now spoke. "Your name is Tiger, right?"

"So what about it?"

"I wanted to ask about a crow that you may have taken a bite or two out of last night."

The cat rolled his eyes. "Great. You *are* a couple of New Age hippies."

It was Krahe's turn to speak again. "Oh no, sir. We hold no offense against you for your natural instincts. It's just that something didn't quite add up about the way the chap was found. We thought maybe you could tell us how he was when you found him." Krahe asked his question in a manner that would allow the cat to lie a bit; he wanted to see if the feline would cover for a killer crow he had made a deal with.

Tiger relaxed a bit, and took another bite out of the mouse. As he chewed, he said, "Well, let's see. He was standin' there... I think he was hunting for worms or whatever it is you guys eat. I came up behind him and pounced."

"And that was all of it?"

"That was it. He barely even had time to squawk. I gave him a bite to the neck, a good, hard death shake," he shook the remainder of the mouse corpse to illustrate, flinging blood and bits of mouse guts around him. "And then I left. I was in the mood for the hunt last night, not the meal. You two want what's left of this mouse?"

Corbeau said, "No thank you. Anything else you remember about last night?"

Tiger began licking his paws and wiping his ears clean. "Not a thing. Mind leaving me to my business now?"

Krahe politely said, "Not at all. Thank you for your time." The two crows took to the air again. During a glide, Krahe said, "He's watching us leave, isn't he?"

Corbeau looked back, then said, "Yes. Yes, he is."

"Alright then. Let's fly off to that grove there, where he can't see us. We'll turn back around at a high altitude and watch where he goes."

The cat's movements took him in a roundabout fashion to a place close to a spot on the river bank where there were no nests. Corbeau whispered to Krahe as they flew high above, "I think I see a crow down there on the ground."

"Yes. It looks as if he's waiting for the cat," Krahe replied.

"Indeed. Curious."

Krahe said, "The cat is an obvious liar. His whiskers twitched ever so much whenever he tried pulling one over on us. I think Hawkins was dead or injured when the cat got to him."

Below them, the cat and bird conferred for a few moments. The bird then took to wing, flying low and slow. Tiger followed through the brush. Krahe said to Corbeau, still in a whisper, "Do you recognize that crow?"

"No. Tough to see any features this late at night." About forty yards away from the meeting point, the crow landed. Corbeau and Krahe could see a flopping form in the grass. It was an injured crow. The two detectives looked at each other. Corbeau, still keeping his voice down despite his excitement, asked, "What do we do?"

Krahe grimaced. "If we fly down there, we're in for an attack. The crow that led Tiger to the injured bird may have cohorts. That injured fellow down there—" the cat sprang on him just then, "He's done. We should follow the other bird, the one that led the cat." Corbeau nodded in agreement.

The bird stayed low, and took a long, roundabout route to a large grove of trees between the edge of town and a plowed field that looked empty of any crops. Once he flew under the cover of the trees, Krahe and Corbeau couldn't see exactly where he went. Corbeau turned to Krahe. "What now? I know that grove; there are a lot of nests. It could be any one of a score of crows."

"Hmm." Krahe thought for a few moments while they glided in wide circles above the trees. "I guess that we should go back to the crow that Tiger finished off."

"Will we be up all night, Krahe? It's very late..."

"Yes, I know. You've got a breakfast date. We'll see what evidence we can get tonight. I think we were lucky with Hawkins that a fox or coyote didn't sniff out his corpse and eat him before he was discovered." They turned and took a straight path back to the spot where the other bird had been killed. It was a much shorter flight when taken directly.

They could see Tiger below them silently making his way through the brush near the area. Krahe said to Corbeau, "He's on his way home now. Had his fun for the night."

They landed close to the body of the crow, and walked through the brush to it. The moonlight was bright, and Krahe immediately pointed to the large crow's wingtip. "By Jove, Corbeau! Look at that!"

"It's Eagle, Krahe. That dead bird is Eagle!"

"His wingtip, old man! Look at it shine in the moonlight." Krahe insisted.

Corbeau leaned in a little closer, and said, "Yes, I see it. Purple. Just like his father and Hawkins. Do you really think it means anything?"

Krahe turned to Corbeau. "It could mean nothing or it could mean everything. It's an identifier, something in common between the victims."

"Nimble showed me his wingtip after the joust today. Said he's only seen it in his bloodline."

Krahe reached out with his foot and turned Eagle's head. He pointed to the dead crow's face and said, "Eyes. Poked out again. Broken wing. We've got ourselves a serial killer who is out to get these brothers."

"Should we alert Gust?"

Krahe shook his head. "Not just yet; I think the killer will only go for one target each night. We'll get to him tomorrow. Everyone else is going to put together that the brothers are targets, just as fast as we did." He jerked his head to the left. "Shhh! What's that?"

The two birds took wing, flying straight up in case a predator was close. Krahe turned to look back, and saw a fox nosing through the brush to Eagle's body. "Look there, Corbeau."

Corbeau stopped his escaping climb and swopped back around, spying the fox. "Do you think that the killer knew a fox would find Eagle out here?"

"I doubt it. The killer would have to take whatever opportunity he had to kill his target. The fox is just luck." They

14

began their flight back to Nightfield as the fox began feeding on Eagle's dead body.

As they approached the river side of the field, Corbeau said to Krahe, "That's my tree just over there. A small nest, but that's all one needs when he's on his own."

"Indeed. My nest is on Turkey Hill. See you there tomorrow for lunch."

"Why not meet here? It's closer to the crime scenes."

"I'd like some privacy so we can talk about what we know so far."

"Alright then. Meet you tomorrow."

***

After Krahe broke off from Corbeau, he began a scenic route back to Turkey Hill. He wanted to see where Tiger was and if the cat was heading straight home or making any other stops along the way. With the moon now higher in the sky than before, it was easy to pick out Tiger on the ground. Krahe watched as the gray cat approached the edge of the last field before the street, then noticed something stalking the cat from about thirty yards behind. It was a coyote!

Krahe swooped down behind the cat and called out loudly, "Tiger! You've got a coyote on your tail! Get home now!"

Tiger, being of typical cat nerve, immediately leapt off into a run. The coyote began bounding after, looking up at Krahe and snarling, "Damn you, crow!"

Krahe swooped toward the coyote, pulling up at a steep angle in front of him. It was enough to slow the coyote down and allow Tiger to get to the houses. Krahe watched as the cat ran to a front door and pawed at it frantically.

A tired-looking human male opened the door to let Tiger in, and the coyote disappeared into the field. The human yawned, stretched, and took in a deep breath of night air, saying, "Hey, boy. You find some action tonight?" Tiger turned, looked at Krahe and smiled, then pranced into the house.

Krahe said to himself, "I believe I've just made a friend. A cat could come in handy some day."

15

Krahe spent the next morning reviewing everything he knew about the case while he waited for Corbeau, and planning how to approach Gust. Krahe had just pulled a chewing twig from his beak and began nibbling at a bit of stale bread, part of his winnings from the previous day's joust, when Corbeau arrived. Krahe smiled. "Hello, old man! Any trouble finding the place?"

"None at all. You're almost the only crow on this part of the hill. A pleasant turkey down there gave me directions."

"I bet it was Roderick."

"I didn't catch his name. He was sitting in the ditch pecking gravel from near the main road. An older gent."

"Yes, that's Roderick, alright. He's practically addicted to gravel, the senile old thing. I keep waiting for the poor fellow to end up in the grill of a car someday. How was breakfast with Lenore?"

"Oh, it was splendid! She's a doll, that one."

"Hmm. Think it will go anywhere?"

Corbeau shrugged. "Don't know. She's a pretty independent gal." Corbeau surveyed the branch where they sat. Krahe's nest, an old thing made up of dried leaves and more bits of twine than the usual nest, sat in a crotch of two branches. Krahe had scribbled notes all over the branch and trunk of the tree about various cases he had worked on.

"So," Corbeau asked, "Which of these scribbles is our case?"

"Ah! These, right over here. I think that today we should talk with Gust and warn him."

"Agreed. I don't know if anyone has found Eagle yet, but after that fox there may not be much to find. I thought about approaching the family this morning, but decided it would be best to talk it over with you first."

"Right." Krahe pointed to some notes. "I also made notes on the modus operandi of our killer."

"I was thinking about that, too. I think he's a large crow," Corbeau said.

Krahe shook his head. "No, he's a smaller fellow. The broken wing that we saw with each victim... I think it had strategic meaning."

"How so?"

"Yesterday, when you jousted Eagle, do you remember that dive that almost put you in the river?"

"Yes, it frightened the daylights out of me."

Krahe nodded his head. "Imagine riding him to the ground, using your smaller body—not that I think you to be small, you understand—to pin one wing so that he couldn't recover from the dive."

Corbeau nodded. "I see. But couldn't a large crow do the same thing?"

"A large crow wouldn't need to pin the wing back and break it. He could just ride the other bird into the dirt and use the force of the crash to shock him," Krahe said.

"So the smaller crow forces the larger one to fall just right..."

"And crack! Next come the eyes. When the larger bird is in shock and pain from the fall, the smaller one pecks his eyes."

"A dreadfully uncivilized thing, that eye pecking." Corbeau replied. "Why does he do it, though? The cat certainly doesn't need the bird to be blinded. A crow with an injured wing, even a big chap like Eagle, would be not much more than a moderate challenge for a cat like Tiger."

Krahe said, "Right. Except that this killer has to find just the right opportunity to tackle his target in mid-air, in the dark, when nobody else is around."

Corbeau nodded. "No telling where the cat would be then."

"Right," Krahe continued, "The cat is insurance. If you or I broke a wing in any field in the area, how long until a random fox, cat, coyote, or other predator found us?"

Corbeau shrugged. "Depends, I guess. Anywhere from a few minutes to a few hours."

"So the killer blinds the victim to make him more susceptible to any passing predator that wants an easy meal. Just in case Tiger can't be found."

Corbeau shivered. "Dreadful. So what do we do now?"

Krahe popped another chunk of stale bread in his mouth, chewed thoughtfully, and said "We find Gust. I'll talk to him. You hang back, and see if you can detect any crows following him."

The day was warm with spring sunlight. Fluffy clouds hung over the flock in the blue sky. To animals with light colored coats, the day was cool. To animals with dark coats, like the black feathers of the crows, the sun was baking hot. Gust, having not seen Eagle all day, was coming to accept that both of the birds who had hatched from the same nest as he did were gone now. Missing this long meant death; Gust was the lone surviving sibling, and he knew it.

Krahe landed next to Gust, and went straight to the point. "Excuse me, Gust. My name is Krahe. I'm a detective."

Gust turned to Krahe and said evenly, "Did someone find him?" His eyes looked dull, sad, and worn with worry.

"Is there a place we can speak in private? It's important."

Gust sighed. "Let's fly."

They took wing and flew south, along the river bank. They took a low altitude, and soon enough had passed out of the range of the rest of the flock. As they set into a glide, Krahe said, "It was actually somewhat close to here where it happened."

"They've found a body?"

"No. But I was following a cat last night who arrived shortly after Eagle was attacked. A crow flew away from the scene." Krahe did not want to go into the whole mess about Tiger being a sort of accomplice. Crows and cats cooperating in murder would be confusing in the least, and could cause a riot if it became public information. Besides, Krahe had a feeling that, despite his association with the murderer, Tiger might be a good ally. There was even a slim chance the cat would give up the name of the killer if pressed, but Krahe didn't think he'd get that lucky.

"I knew it!" Gust said. "Was it the same one who killed Hawkins, do you think? He must be a mighty bird to take down Eagle."

"I think it was the same killer for both brothers, yes." Krahe replied. "But I don't know who it is. I feel that you are in

18

danger, Gust. Is there anyone who might have it out for you and your brothers? A jousting rival, perhaps?"

Gust shook his head. "No. No one. We're fierce in the joust, but after that we're just like any other crows. We gamble, we hunt, we play sticks and stones."

"Hmm. Any of you married?"

Again, Gust shook his head. "No. Hawkins was courting a girl, and Eagle had a wife for two years who was killed in a bad storm last summer. I've been too busy enjoying the single life. I promised my father I'd meet him for lunch, can we turn around now?"

"Yes, of course." As they changed course, Krahe said, "So no romantic rivals, then?"

Gust shook his head. "None for any of us."

They returned to the flock, and Gust left to meet his father. Krahe expected Corbeau to join him any minute, but the crow was absent. Krahe waited and waited, and eventually, the sun passed in its long arc overhead and began to lay low in the west. Krahe had a bad feeling about Corbeau, and he decided to do some searching, afraid the killer had spotted the young detective following him, and done him in.

Krahe took off and flew the route that he and Gust had taken earlier. If the killer had followed Gust, and noticed that Corbeau was, in turn, following him, he most likely would have turned on Corbeau sometime on that route. Krahe saw no signs of a fight, no loose feathers, no downed birds. He turned to loop back to Nightfield.

On the southeast edge of the field, Krahe could see some sort of ruckus involving about twenty birds. He landed in one of the trees the birds occupied, and listened to Visto, the trouble-making New Age crow as he paced back and forth on the ground. Visto seemed very agitated, and crows in the crowd cheered him on until he finally began to speak.

"Brothers and sisters," he began, "Now is the time to take our rightful place! Now is the time to hold predators and humans accountable for the deaths of our fellow crows!" He stopped for cheers and applause, then continued. "We need true leadership to do this. The Council of Intelligence is no government. We crows have never banded together under a single leader, and it is time, I say. Time for a *revolution*!" More cheers and applause. Krahe felt a tap on his shoulder. He turned and almost jumped with excitement at the sight. There was Corbeau!

He smiled wide and bowed low to show his happiness. "Corbeau! I thought for a minute there I'd lost you!"

Corbeau smiled back. "Still here, my friend. I found something that you may want to see." Corbeau led Krahe to another tree, under the canopy where they had watched the killer disappear the night before. "I came in here to do some poking around once I realized that nobody was following Gust." They hopped from branch to branch, until they were on a high branch that overlooked four nests. "Look at that nest there, the one with the clutch of one-year old chicks."

Krahe observed the nest, and said in a curious manner, "Do I see purple wing tips on those young birds?"

"You do indeed, Krahe. You'll never believe who their father—well the husband of their mother—is."

"Who?"

"The leader of the New Age movement against predators, Visto."

"The killer who uses a cat to finish the job for him is the very crow leading the movement to consider cat preying on crows murder! By Jove! And he's killing those brothers because he knows they are the only crows around with purple wing tips."

"Right. He can not only take revenge on whichever of them had an affair with his wife, but also try to rile up hatred toward our natural predators."

Krahe whistled through his teeth. "That's quite the scheme."

"Who do we go to first, Gust or the Council of Intelligence," Corbeau asked.

"Sun's almost down. I think we need to talk to Gust and find out which brother fathered those chicks."

"Right." They took wing toward the tree that Gust and his brothers had all nested in. When they were close to the tree, they saw a crow fly from it. Krahe turned to Corbeau and said, "That's Gust. After our talk today, I can't believe he's leaving the safety of his tree this close to darkness!"

They flew as fast as they could to catch up to Gust. When they did, Krahe asked him, "Gust, what in the world are you doing? I told you, there is someone out to kill you."

"Yes," Gust replied, "And I want him to come for me. Now peel off, so that he can find me alone and I can take care of this myself."

"But Gust," Corbeau said, "We've identified the killer. We can go to the Council and tell them our evidence. He'll be put to death for what he's done."

Gust set his wings and coasted for a moment, thinking about this. Then he said, "No. I'll kill him myself." He kept pumping his wings.

"His name is Visto," Krahe said, "And he has chicks about one year old with purple wing tips. They obviously were fathered by one of your family. He must not know who, because he's killing each of you."

Gust shook his head. "Couldn't be. I've never mated. Eagle had mated with his wife, but after she died he said he would never mate again. Hawkins... well, he and I shared everything. He would have told me."

Krahe pointed to a tree below. "Let's land on that tree and sort this thing out. The longer you're in the air, the longer you're a target." When they were on the branch, Krahe paced back and forth. "So we have offspring that very obviously came from your family, but none of your brothers or you could have fathered them."

Gust nodded. "Right."

Corbeau said, "It's a good thing you didn't find Visto tonight, Gust. If he was powerful enough to take down Eagle, I think it might have been trouble for you."

Gust shrugged, and said, "I was upset. Thank you fellows, for talking with me. Look, why don't I go back to my family's tree while you go to the Council. They can order the arrest while I explain things to—"

"Your father!" Krahe shouted. "Does your father tell you everything the way Hawkins did, Gust?"

Gust shook his head. "No, he's actually quite a private crow. Never has been very caring towards us brothers beyond training us for the joust. If it weren't for the wealth he's given us from the jousting business, well, I think that the three of us would have moved away from him long ago."

Krahe looked Gust in the eyes, and said "He's not just *your* father, Gust."

"The chicks!" Gust exclaimed.

Corbeau nodded. "Of course! Krahe, nice work. Nobody would have suspected Nimble of having an affair. He's got a good reputation and is seen as a family man. He's no rogue, living single and refusing to mate. No offense at that rogue thing, Gust, but you get my meaning."

Gust nodded. "Of course."

Krahe said, "Alright, then. Gust, you should fly with us. Visto will be less likely to attack you if you aren't alone. We'll go first to the Council, then to Nimble."

Gust kicked at the branch, grimaced, and said, "No! I'm going to confront my father. He's gotten his own children killed. And my poor mother! What is she going to think!" With that, Gust hopped off the branch and took wing.

Krahe turned to Corbeau, "We need to follow him and keep him safe."

"Right!" Corbeau and Krahe took off. It was already dark enough that finding Gust was difficult. Once Corbeau spotted him, he saw a shape flying above Gust. It must be Visto!

Corbeau turned to Krahe and said, "There! Above Gust!" Corbeau then pumped his wings to cut the distance between himself and Gust, simultaneously gaining altitude, hoping to possibly intercept the other bird. Corbeau watched as Visto climbed a bit, then dove straight for Gust.

Corbeau changed his angle of attack. He was already at his top speed and could only hope to stop the attack by ramming Visto mid-dive. As Visto plummeted toward Gust, Corbeau sprinted toward a point just above where he judged the collision would take place. Sure enough, just a second before Visto would have slammed into Gust and taken him to the ground to break a wing, Corbeau and Visto collided.

They tumbled toward the ground, both knocked woozy from the collision. Corbeau was dizzy and felt like the wind had been knocked out of him. As his head cleared, he heard Gust shouting at him as he tried to dive alongside the two falling crows. "Corbeau! Corbeau! Wake up, man! You're falling!"

Corbeau set out his wings and recovered from the tumble and into a glide just twenty feet from the ground. He heard a sickening *thud* as Visto impacted. Gust and Corbeau landed near the crumpled body of Visto. Krahe landed just after.

The injured bird lay unmoving on the ground before them, huffing for breath. He looked around, but nothing on his body moved except for his head. He said nothing. It was obvious that he was dying. Corbeau asked, "Is there anything we can do, Visto?"

Visto opened his beak to speak, but no words came out. His breaths became more and more shallow and rapid, until they stopped and he stared upward to the stars, dead. Gust turned to Krahe and Corbeau. "We should tell my father. The bastard deserves to know what he's caused."

Krahe nodded. "Yes. The Council will want to know what happened as well."

Gust turned to Corbeau and asked, "Are you injured? That was one epic collision!"

Corbeau smiled. "Nothing a bit of ginger and a good night's sleep won't cure. But I would appreciate it if we can fly slowly to your father; I'm a bit sore."

***

Corbeau and Krahe ate lunch in Corbeau's nest a week later. "Lenore says hello, by the way," Corbeau said.

"She's a sweet lady, Corbeau. You should really think about making her a permanent fixture. This nest is too big for one."

Corbeau smiled. "We'll see what happens." They pecked at some grubs, still enjoying the winnings of the joust bets Krahe had placed on Corbeau. They heard a noise of the ground below, and looked over the side of the nest. It was Tiger.

23

"Tiger," Corbeau said, "What are you doing here?"

The cat sat, flicked his tail, and asked, "Are you two for hire?"

Krahe and Corbeau looked at each other, then turned back to Tiger. Krahe asked, "What do you mean, *for hire?*"

Tiger looked around, as if a bit embarrassed. "Well, it's just... one of my friends was eaten by a coyote. Thing is, this cat never, I mean *never* went in Nightfield. I think someone led him to the coyote to be killed."

Krahe winked at Corbeau and whispered, "We're set, old man. As long as you love solving the puzzles, you've got a job with me." Corbeau smiled and nodded.

Krahe leaned out of the nest and called down to the cat, "We'll take it."

Jenny on the Milk Carton

Brian Page was more or less hypnotized by the machine in front of him. It wound hundreds of small fibers around each other until they were tight. Those tight fibers, having been braided together into thin orange twine, then wrapped around a cylinder until they were a bale. Brian would cut the end off, remove the bale from the cylinder, and slide it into a machine that wrapped plastic around the twine and heated it until it shrunk around the bale, making it a complete package. It was boring. It was easy. It was more or less mindless. It was perfect for a man who wanted nothing more in life than to go to his happy place, his mental garden of Zen, his pool of imagination, and swim into stories he spun for himself.

He would make up stories about the people around him, mostly. There was Cob, the old geezer with so many tattoos up and down his arms that when he wore short sleeves it looked like his skin was really made of ornately patterned silk. Cob operated another bailer. Then Gina, a plump twenty-year-old who graduated high school with Brian's younger brother Larry. She loaded the machines that started braiding the individual fibers together. Finally was Vern, the only black guy around for about a hundred miles. He was quiet, his body a weird sort of muscle-fat combination that made him look both oafish and ogrish, and he had a branding scar on his right arm. He drove the forklift that brought in the large round coils of fiber. The empty pallets were then brought to the back side of the line, and Vern would stack the bales of packaged twine on them and drive the pallets to the warehouse to be shipped out.

They worked the midnight shift together. The warehouse and offices were empty during this shift, and the four of them more or less had the run of the facility. Officially, the afternoon shift supervisor Roy was also their supervisor, although they only saw him twice a year. Once on clean-up day, and once on annual review day.

Brian's stories for Cob usually centered around Cob as a sailor in World War II. Brian knew that Cob was too young for that, but with all those tattoos, and how damn skinny the old guy was, it just seemed to fit. Brian could see Cob as a twenty-year old, manning a huge machine gun as Kamikazes flew in toward him, the pilots shouting "*Toraaaaaaaaaa!*" It was all quite dramatic to Brian. A few times, he'd picture the WWII version of Cob stranded on an island, watching his ship sink in the distance. Other times, he pictured him fending off sharks while he waited for rescue like the story the cool dude in *Jaws* told. A few times when he'd imagine Cob on the deserted island, a few native girls in grass skirts and no tops would wander into the story, then Brian had to change things so that it was himself who was stranded and not Cob. Otherwise it could get weird.

His stories about Gina were mostly trailer park Jerry Springer stuff, and Brian felt bad, because he knew that her life pretty much *was* trailer park Jerry Springer stuff. She already had two kids from two different guys. Now and then, she'd show up to work with a shiner, and Brian would imagine what must have happened. He'd picture four guys in the living room, arguing over who was the father of the baby in the room down the hall. None of them were arguing that they *were* the father, but all of them would point to each other and say "He did it! I'd never touch her!"

The stories for Vern were Brian's favorite. Brown skin is a rarity in northwestern North Dakota. Living in a town that was in sight of the Canadian border did wonders for Brian's imagination when it came to Vern. He'd picture Vern as The Black Mounty, riding into drug busts on a jet black horse, and saying cool action hero lines in a crazy Canadian/Ebonics dialect, things like "*You hosers axed for it, eh!*" Before blasting a bunch of French-Canadian drug lords to hell. Other times, he'd picture Vern on the other end of things, being the biggest, baddest, bad-ass in a prison. In these fantasies, Vern was so bad, he'd take over the warden's office as his own and make the warden do his work in Vern's assigned cell.

He was in the middle of one of these daydreams at about three in the morning when he heard Gina scream in horror. He snapped awake and looked over to her. She was just standing there, pointing to Cob's machine and screaming, tears squirting from her eyes. Vern drove in from the warehouse as Brian looked over to where Cob should be standing. He saw Cob's feet sticking out of the baler, turning in circles. Brian knew that inside the machine, the old man would be mangled, wound into a bale of twine.

All Brian could do was stand there and try not to pee his pants while Gina screamed and cried. As soon as Vern saw what was happening, he was off the forklift and running to the bailer. He punched the large, red emergency stop button hard enough to crack the case of the machine. He looked down into the baling mechanism, turned around, and vomited all over the floor.

They gave the midnight crew three days off. The funeral was the next Saturday. Closed casket, of course. Brian wore the best clothes he had, a black and gray plaid shirt, black jeans, a faded brown leather belt, and his work shoes, which didn't look too bad after a polish and some brown paint where the steel toe was showing through the leather.

The three remaining members of the midnight shift sat close together in the church. Gina cried, Vern fiddled with his thumbs, and Brian watched to see who was there. When Cob's wife went up front to say a few words, Brian finally learned that Cob had indeed served in the Navy. Vietnam. Two tours. The local bikers were all there, and Brian figured that must explain the tattoos.

Dinner after the funeral was at Cob's house. It was a small place, one of the tiny houses built in the fifties when it was cool to make every residence in the neighborhood look exactly alike, and entire families could pack themselves into about eight hundred square feet of American dream. Roy sauntered up to Brian, Gina, and Vern as they stood around a table of snacks, munching and chatting.

He rubbed his mustache with his thumb and pointer finger, and propped up on the balls of his feet a couple of times. "So. You three are going to get a new coworker soon. I expect that whoever we hire will get trained in right."

Vern nodded. "Maybe we can talk about that at work, Roy."

Roy twitched the corner of his mouth, obviously annoyed. "There's no more to talk about." His voice sounded as skinny as his old-man body. He flushed with embarrassment just a bit, which actually made him look better. Instead of pale and sallow, he suddenly looked just a touch pink. "One last thing. We had an OSHA visit while you three were off. We're going to install the clam tops back onto the machines." He looked to all three of them, turned on his heels, and walked away into the crowd of about twenty other people who crammed into the small house. Outside, a loud motorcycle roared by.

Vern looked at Brian and Gina. "What a jerk. You know they gave us those days off so that we couldn't talk to OSHA."

Brian shrugged. He actually hadn't ever thought of that. Gina groaned a bit, put her hand on her stomach, and shuffled away. Brian sighed, and asked Vern, "So when do you think the new person will start?"

"Brian, I don't think Cob is even in the ground yet." They stared at each other for a few silent moments, and Vern finally added, "A week. Tops."

It was more like two weeks before Roy was waiting with a new employee one night when Brian arrived for his shift. The old man stood in front of the machine—now equipped with a plastic cover over the top. Next to Roy stood a woman about Brian's age. She was short and so petite that she appeared to be almost dangerously skinny. Her blond hair was cut really short; Brian thought he had heard that style called a "pixie cut" once on TV. He was immediately interested in her, but tried to act casual.

Roy kept things short, as usual. "Brian, this is Jenny. She's going to operate Cob's baler. Teach her how and keep an eye on her until she knows what she's doing." With that, he walked off to punch out and leave for home.

Brian stuck out his hand to shake, and said, "Hi. I'm Brian."

Jenny smiled politely and shook Brian's hand. It was brief. Her grip was very loose, her skin very cold. She said nothing, and immediately after the handshake, looked away from Brian. He walked over to his operating station, and asked "Did Roy show you anything yet?"

She shook her head and said in a quiet, tiny voice, "He, um, no. We just... All I did was paperwork. I don't know anything."

"Okay. Well, here's the basics." He pointed out controls and what each one did. When Gina and Vern got there, he introduced them to Jenny. She barely said a word. The first two hours of the shift, she watched the way Brian operated his baler. Then they went over to hers, and she began running it. She was very tentative at first. Instead of asking a question when she was unsure about something, she would delicately reach for the control she wondered about, then pull her hand back, then reach out for it again. After doing this a few times, she would look at Brian. Again, she said nothing. Brian would say things like, "Yeah, that's the button to press," or "Not yet. You have to wait until the bale is done winding."

By lunch time, she had figured things out well enough to work completely on her own for a half hour. Lunch was at four AM sharp every day. Brian shut down his machine, then showed Jenny how to shut her baler down. She stepped back and looked at him questioningly. He smiled at her and said, "Lunch. Did you bring anything?"

She hinted at a smile, and nodded. "I, uh... I packed," she paused, "I, I packed a um, a sandwich." When she finished the words, she smiled more, as if she were relieved the sentence was finally over.

"Cool. Vern goes home for lunch every day, and Gina usually walks to the gas station. It'll be nice to have someone to talk to."

They walked together to the lunch room while Vern and Gina wandered out of the building. Brian stuck his mom's leftover green bean hot dish in the microwave and started it, then went to the pop machine and got a drink. He sat at the grimy lunch table across from Jenny, who had a brown sack in front of her. She had already taken out her sandwich, and had filled a Styrofoam cup with water from the lunchroom sink. He looked at her while she chewed on a bite of sandwich and tried to think of what to talk about. Here he was, having a meal alone with a pretty girl. He couldn't let the opportunity get away from him.

"So, Jenny, I've never seen you around. Do you live in town?"

She shook her head and swallowed her bite of sandwich. "I live, um, my... me and my dad live," another of those odd pauses she seemed have, "We uh, live on a farm. Out of town."

"Oh." The microwave beeped, and Brian took out his leftovers and sat back down. "Did you always live there?"

She shook her head again. "Only about six months."

They ate silently for a few moments. "What kind of sandwich do you have? It looks good." Brian was lying. The sandwich, white bread with the crusts ripped off, some mayo, mustard, and a few slices of deli meat, looked terrible and boring. He just needed to say something. The silence felt odd.

Jenny smiled at him. "Ham." She blushed a little, and took another bite. The rest of their lunch break was filled with Brian talking about himself, since Jenny was more or less the vow of silence type. When a half hour was up, he stood and said, "Well, back to work. Any questions so far?"

Jenny shook her head, folded the sandwich baggie and paper sack up into small squares, and stuck them both in her back pocket. She followed Brian to the work floor, where Vern was arriving back. He smiled at the two of them and said, "You two pals yet?"

Brian just about tripped over his own toes when Jenny smiled, nodded her head, and said, "Yeah."

He watched her from his baler for the rest of the night. She was so thin and petite that her clothes hung around her, only hinting at the shape beneath. Brian still couldn't help but try to imagine what her body would look like, first in more form-fitting clothes, then moving on to underwear, and finally complete nudity. He tried to hide behind his machine when she would turn to smile and wave hello every hour or so, because he was afraid that she would see the way his pants had tightened in front.

Gina left the work floor five times in the last half of the shift, and Brian noticed the dark circles under her eyes. He had known her long enough to know when she was pregnant. He wondered who the father was *this* time, or if she even knew. When

30

eight rolled around and the four of them gathered at the time clock to punch out, Vern turned to the group and said "How about breakfast?"

Brian nearly jumped up and down. "Yeah! We haven't done breakfast in a long time!"

Gina chimed in with "Sure. I don't feel like getting the kids ready for school anyway. Mom can do it today."

Vern looked at Jenny. "How about you, Jenny? We'd like to get to know you."

Brian was happy Vern had the idea for breakfast. He was the only social one of the group, really. Jenny looked to Gina and Brian, shrugged, and said, "I guess so. I um, my..." a pause, "I have to call Dad first."

Vern smiled and nodded. "Sure. Wouldn't want him to get worried about you on your first day. You know where the Magic Chef is?" Jenny nodded. "Okay. When you get off the phone with your dad, come down there." He walked off, Gina following close behind.

Brian walked out to his car and watched as the day shift crew arrived. This was the shift that had all the office people; this shift also ran all seven balers instead of just the two that ran during midnights. There were about forty people who worked days. Brian could have switched to the day or afternoon shift a year ago, but he liked nights. He could sleep when his parents were home, and a lot of the people on day shift were the same people that had been cruel to him in high school. He pretended to be fiddling with his radio until he saw Jenny come outside to her car.

Brian stepped out of his beat-up early nineties Chevy and walked over to the beat-up early nineties Honda that Jenny was about to get in to. "So, you know how to get there, right?"

She nodded. "I can, um, follow you, though. I mean, you know" a pause, "If you want to go, um, well, together. Maybe."

Brian smiled. "Yeah, that sounds good."

When they got to the restaurant, a square glass place that had a statue out front of a chef in a poufy French hat flipping pancakes with a magic wand, Gina was outside on her phone arguing with her mother about getting the kids ready for school,

31

and having a smoke. As they passed by, she stopped arguing and said, "Vern got us a table already." She went back to her phone to continue the argument with, "I don't give a shit, Mom, just give 'em toast or something. It's only breakfast."

Brian said awkwardly, "Okay. Thanks." He and Jenny walked into the restaurant that was populated with one group of local farmers having coffee and playing dice, and one Vern sitting alone in a corner booth. Brian and Jenny joined him. Brian flushed a bit when Jenny slid into the seat next him, looked at him shyly, and smiled.

Vern smiled at her. "Jenny, tell me about yourself. How old are you?"

"Um, twenty, uh, oh I guess about twenty-six."

Vern looked confused. "*About* twenty-six?"

"Well, um, I was born, uh" she paused, looking away to the blue sky out the window then back again, "You know, I'm twenty-six." Gina sat down next to Vern, yawned, and opened a menu.

Vern continued. "Any brothers or sisters? When did you and your dad move here?"

She shook her head. "Nobody else. We came here, um, I guess this is a place, well... I don't know. Dad just came here."

Brian asked, "Where's your mom?"

Jenny looked out the window and said simply, "Dead." The conversation quieted from there, and after a few minutes, Vern, Gina, and Brian gossiped about people on the day and afternoon shifts.

The next night at work was also quiet. Brian watched Jenny again, and started to make up new stories, this time starring her. In his first, she was secretly an actress on the verge of huge fame and fortune, working at the twine factory to research a role. In this daydream, under her frumpy sweater and baggie jeans, she wore silk and lace underwear adorned with jewels, so that she could feel Hollywood luxury on her body even as she posed as a poor working girl. That got him started thinking about her body again, and by the end of the story it was nothing but thoughts that completely distracted him from his work.

On their first fifteen-minute break, Gina went outside to have a cigarette, and Vern made a phone call. Jenny and Brian sat on a bench outside watching Gina smoke. Brian leaned toward Jenny and said, "I think you might be the shortest grown-up person I know."

She giggled a little, and replied, "I'm five four. There was, um, at the last place I lived, this girl." She stopped talking for almost a full minute before starting again. "This girl, you know… she was, like four ten or something."

"Wow. That's pretty short."

"Yeah. But she still weighed more than me. I weigh ninety-five pounds."

"That's skinny."

They were back to work soon after, and Brian's mind wandered almost immediately into another story about Jenny. In this one, a top secret government agency comes to town looking for her. They need to draft her back into service after a retirement from the spy life, because they have to sneak into a terrorist base, and the only way in is through a narrow vent shaft. Brian pictures her training to fight and shoot weapons, all while wearing short-shorts and a tank top. Then, when the mission is about to start, they discover that the base is wired with hundreds of booby-traps, all tied to snares with orange twine. The only twine specialist they can get on such short notice is Brian. They train him and give him drugs to build his muscles, so instead of the five foot seven guy who weighs a buck sixty with a beer gut, he's built like that Russian guy in *Rocky 3*. Or was that *Rocky 4*? He couldn't remember.

Either way, they go on their mission. Brian makes it through all the booby traps, nearly getting blown to bits time after time. Jenny saves him once by ripping off her tank top and wrapping it around a detonator, so now she's just in a sheer bra. With jewels. They get to the vent, and the only way she'll fit is if he rubs a specially engineered oil all over her body. It's going to be so tight, that even the short-shorts have to go, and now she's just in a tiny red thong while he rubs her down with oil… It was the one and only night that Brian ever relieved himself at work, and he vowed never to let a story get away from him like that again.

He was very quiet at lunch time. They sat across from each other, the only sounds their biting, chewing, and sips of pop from cans. When it was only about a minute before lunch was going to end, Jenny broke the silence. "Um. Do you... I mean, if I..." she stopped and huffed out air from her mouth, closed her eyes tight, and spoke with her eyelids clamped shut. The words came out so fast that Brian almost didn't understand them. "If I bring you a sandwich tomorrow will you eat it?" She kept her eyes shut as hard as she could shut them, and turned red with embarrassment.

Brian cleared his throat, reached across the table, and gently wrapped his hand around her fingers. "I'd like that."

When he got home that morning, the house was, as usual, empty. His dad was off to work at the garage, and his mom was off to work at the small fast food counter inside the gas station. Larry was never home, and Brian assumed he was still out at a party from the night before. His day at home was typical, boring, and long. He crawled into bed in his large basement bedroom at about three in the afternoon. He'd wake up at eleven, take a shower and eat breakfast, then leave for work. It was going to be nice out, so he thought maybe he'd ride his bike to work the next night.

His parents woke him up at about nine, arguing about the phone bill. Through the floor, he could hear them going back and forth about who called whom, and who used up all their minutes. Brian was glad he had finally gotten his own damn phone, so he didn't need to be a part of those arguments any more. Why couldn't they just be quiet and go to sleep? He tossed and turned until his alarm went off. The whole time he was trying to sleep, he kept thinking about Jenny. He'd have to pretend to like the sandwich, no matter what.

When Jenny arrived at work, she was extra quiet, didn't say hello to Brian, and went directly to her machine to start it up. He watched her, making up stories that were tamer, like one where she was really there because she used to be a nanny for a mob boss, and was in a witness protection program.

When lunchtime came around, Jenny walked silently to the lunchroom, and Brian followed. She smiled at him, and said, "Will you um, get us some pop?"

34

"Sure." He knew exactly what she liked. Generic orange pop. Brian liked the grape kind, and could never figure out why Vern always called it *Knee High*, even though its real name was nothing like that. When he sat down across from Jenny, he noticed that she was bouncing in her chair with nerves. She took two sandwiches out of the same paper bag she's brought in since her first day, and slid one over to Brian. He could see that it was packed with lots of extra meat and still had the crust. Jenny bit her bottom lip and smiled at him. "Um, I thought, you know. You're a guy and stuff. So, uh, more... More meat." She paused, and added, "Guys eat more."

He smiled at her, and said "Thanks." She stared at him. It was obvious that she wasn't going to eat until he started. He picked up the sandwich, but when he was about to take a bite, she looked away and held her breath. He bit in and chewed; it was actually pretty good. He made a *mmm* sound, and she turned to face him, a huge smile on her face. She was so happy that her eyes looked wet.

"You like it?" It was the first time she had issued a normal sentence from her mouth in the entire time Brian had known Jenny. He smiled at her and nodded, then took another bite. She bit into her sandwich, and for a while they ate quietly together.

When they had finished, Jenny took the plastic baggie back from Brian, shook the crumbs out of it, and neatly folded it with hers. Then, as she always did, she folded the paper bag, and stuck the items in her back pocket. Brian said, "Maybe tomorrow I can bring us some chips or something."

Jenny nodded, and said, "I'd like that." They stood up to punch back in at the time clock, and Brian held Jenny's hand for a moment. She smiled at him, and he leaned in, gently planting a kiss on her lips. When he drew back again, her eyes were wide, and she pressed her lips together tightly. She swallowed, turned on her heels, punched in, and quickly walked back to her machine. There was little to nothing she did that made any sense to Brian.

Friday. Brian didn't realize until he got to work that he should probably ask Jenny out on a date. With her odd behavior, he was a little bit afraid to. He waited until lunch, when they were sitting quietly across from each other at the grimy table again. "Jenny, do you want to see a movie tomorrow night?"

She looked around the room, as if there might be another Jenny there that Brian was talking to. She leaned in close and said quietly, "There's no theater in town," as if this fact was unknown to him, and may be the cause of embarrassment.

"Well, I meant at my house. I live with my parents, but I have a really big room with a couch and TV and stuff. I have a ton of DVD's."

She sat straight up in her chair, and looked around the empty room again. "But… Brian. Your room? I mean, you know, um…"

"Oh, I don't mean for it to be, you know…" He felt himself turning red. "It's just the only space I've got to myself. We could watch a movie at your house if you want."

Jenny's shoulder's dropped. "My dad." She shook her head. "I can't go out… with people. Guys."

"You're twenty-six."

She shook her head again. "He doesn't like guys."

"So tell him you're working an extra shift, or hanging out with a girl from work."

She leaned forward and said in a secretive tone, "I can't *lie!*" She sat back in her chair, looked at Brian with narrowed eyes, and said, "You're a *bad boy*, aren't you!"

Brian smiled, tried to act cool, and said, "You know it." He pointed at her like his finger was a gun, clicked his tongue a couple of times and winked. In the end, there was no date that weekend. Brian ended up staying in his basement alone while his parents and Larry all went out to the bars. Brian never could understand how a town with eight hundred people could have five bars.

The next few weeks went on this way. Kisses after lunch, mostly small. Every now and then, though, Jenny would push her face hard into Brian's lips, part her lips, and send her tongue into his mouth. He never knew what to expect with her. She refused every invitation to go on a date, but would go out to breakfast once a week; only once, and never more.

It was on one of these ordinary days, as Brian was getting ready for work, that he found Jenny's picture in the most peculiar place. He woke up at eleven, like usual, and was sitting at the kitchen table eating a bowl of generic fruit-flavored cereal, when Larry walked in the door. He was high, and Brian could smell the pot on him as soon as he sat at the table with an empty bowl. Larry nodded to Brian and said, "Hey, Bro."

"Hey." Brian watched Larry fill the bowl with yellow, green, orange, and blue sugary circles, then stare at it as if he wasn't sure what to do next. Brian offered, "Milk?" Larry looked up at him, nodded, and grabbed the carton from the fridge. He poured some into his bowl, took a big drink from the mouth of the carton, and set it down between himself and Brian.

There she was. Under a banner that said, "Have you seen me?" On the left was a picture of a little girl. Cute. Blond. Beneath that picture read "Abigail Richards, born 5/27/1986. Missing since 9/9/1995." On the right was a picture of Jenny. Underneath Jenny's picture it said, "Age progressed photo of Abigail today."

Brian's mouth dropped open. He pointed to the milk carton. "Larry! That's her! That's Jenny!"

"What? No it isn't."

"You've never seen her."

"The mystery chick you claim to make out with at work? No. Never seen her. And you haven't made out with a chick since the last time you were at a party and one passed out." Larry laughed at his joke, then added, "Hey, speaking of that, did you hear that Gina is pregnant again?"

"Yeah. Why?"

"It's just like her first one again. She passed out at a party. The dad could be like, eight different guys."

"Yeah, sure." Brian grabbed the milk carton, walked to the sink, and poured the milk down the drain.

Larry protested, "Hey! Mom's gonna be pissed you wasted the milk."

Brian reached in his pocket, fished out a five dollar bill, and handed it to Larry. "Here, tell her she can go buy more." As he raced down to his room with the milk carton, Larry slyly slipped the five into his own pocket.

When Brian got to work, he wasn't sure what to do. He watched as Jenny walked into the building, looked over to him and smiled. She waved as she walked by to her machine. With shaking hands, he turned his machine on and began his shift.

When they went into the lunchroom at four, she set her bag on the table, turned, and aggressively kissed Brian as he was about to pass by on his way to the pop machine. She smiled and said, "I missed you." Since they had become friends, Brian noticed that Jenny spoke more clearly. There were fewer of those odd pauses, and she tended to look at people's faces more often as she spoke. He got their pops from the vending machine, and sat down across from her. Brian reached into his back pocket, and pulled out the back panel of the milk carton that he had cut away in his room before he left for work.

Without a word, he set it on the table, facing Jenny, and slid it across to her. She suddenly looked very afraid. She bit her lips together until they were white, took a few deep breaths, and said, "She, um, looks kind of... you know... like me a little."

"You're the right age."

"It isn't me."

Gently, and ready for her to say anything in response, Brian asked, "Where are you from, Jenny?"

"We, um, we moved here. From Idaho."

"This little girl was from Iowa."

"It isn't me." A pause, and then, as if he may have forgotten it, she added, "I'm from Idaho."

"She looks a lot like you."

Jenny stood from her chair and turned away from Brian. She walked to the corner and stood facing away from him, her hands by her mouth. He stood, approached her gently, and asked her, "Is it really your dad you live with?"

She shook her head. "It isn't me."

"Okay. I didn't mean to scare you."

She turned and started hitting him with her balled up fists, and screamed "It isn't me it isn't me it isn't me IT ISN'T ME!" Brian tried to get away from her attack, but she kept coming at him, screaming and crying and punching. Finally, he grabbed her in a bear hug. She tried to fight away from him but couldn't. Jenny broke down into full-fledged bawling.

She put herself back together in time for the shift to start again, but wouldn't say a word to Brian. After work, he approached her in the parking lot, but she punched him in the side of the head when he got close, then jumped in her car and drove off. Brian was afraid she and her "father" would leave town and he would never see her again.

But the next night, there she was. She walked into work, ignored Brian as she walked by, and turned on her machine. At lunch time, she only had one sandwich in her bag, and Brian ended up eating a candy bar. He tried to talk to her, but she wouldn't say a word back to him. Two more nights like this, then it was Saturday.

His basement room was quiet, except for the movie he watched, a horror flick that was playing on cable. He heard the doorbell ring, and went up to answer. As usual, everyone else was at the bars. When he swung the door open, Jenny stood there. Her arms were crossed, and she looked down to the ground. Her voice was sullen and almost like that of an angry child. "I wanna come in."

"Okay." Brian stepped aside. Before coming in, she looked at him suspiciously. She walked in with caution. Brian noticed that instead of her usual sweatshirt and jeans, she wore a tee shirt and cut offs. He knew he should just focus on her emotions, but he couldn't help notice how pleasant her legs looked. It was good to finally see them. "Are you hungry?"

Arms still crossed, and lip stuck out in a pout, she nodded. "Do you have a frozen pizza?"

"Yeah, sure." He turned on the oven, pulled a pizza out of the freezer, and set it on the counter. They stared at each other. "I'm really sorry, Jenny. I didn't mean to make you scared or anything. I mean, it probably just looks like you."

"I don't want to talk about it. I want to watch a movie."

"Oh." He was relieved. Maybe she would settle down a bit once they ate and sat on the couch. "Cool. After I put the pizza in, I'll show you my DVD collection. What kind of movies do you like?"

She shrugged. "I have to watch old movies at home all the time. And..." She stopped, lowered her arms to her sides, then said, "Just, um, something new."

"Okay. I have one that just came out last week. It reminds me of Cob. The guy you replaced. It's about World War Two."

"He fought in World War Two?"

"Well, no. But it just reminds me of him."

"Oh." They stared at each other again, until the oven beeped to tell them it was preheated for the pizza.

Half an hour later they sat next to each other on his couch. She was impressed with how big his room was; it looked to her like a living room and bedroom all in one space. She looked around and said, "This is the best place I've ever been in. You can sleep here, hang out here. You never have to leave."

Brian set his plate on the old coffee table that sat in front of them. It was second hand, and had chew marks from a long ago dog. He turned to her. She smiled. He said, "I'm glad you feel better. You can come over here any time you want to, Jenny." He leaned forward and kissed her. She leaned back, pulling him down to the couch cushions with her. They kissed until their hands found the seams of each other's clothes, then peeled the layers away.

When they were finished making love, they lay side-by-side on the couch together. Jenny faced Brian, tears running down her cheeks. He asked, "Are you okay?"

She nodded. He wiped one tear from her cheek, and said, "I've only been with a couple of girls. Neither of them cried. Are you sure you're okay?" She nodded again, began crying more, and buried her face into his chest.

When she was finished crying, she said, "I have to pee."

"Yeah, me too. I'll show you where the bathroom is." The cleaned up together, and Brian dished them both some ice cream. When they were finished, she looked across the kitchen table to him.

"Can I stay here tonight? With you?"

40

Brian smiled. "I'd like that. You won't get in trouble?"

She looked away. "I don't care." Later, they held each other in Brian's bed until they fell asleep. Every time Brian woke up, he changed position to be next to her, to feel her warmth, to try and match the rhythm of his breathing to the rhythm of hers. He wanted her to feel safe.

When he woke and opened his eyes the next morning, her face was right in front of his, eyes wide open. It startled him, and he jumped back a bit. She giggled, leaned toward him, and kissed him. The kissing led to more kissing, and they made love again.

As they lay in the sheets together afterward, she used the sheets to dry the tears from her cheeks. "I want to tell you a secret," she said softly. 'You, um... you can't." She closed her eyes tight, the same way she had when she asked Brian if he would eat a sandwich she made, then said quickly, "You have to promise not to tell anyone no matter what."

"Okay."

She opened her eyes, and more tears ran down her cheeks. "He, um, he isn't really. I mean, I don't think. My dad. Isn't, really." She dabbed tears away again with the sheet. "I don't think."

Brain said, "So then—"

She stuck her palm over his mouth, and said, "More."

Jenny swallowed hard, closed her eyes, and pulled the pillow up over her face so only her mouth was showing. "He's bad to me. Um, you know... really bad. Bad things. He touches... other things. Bad things." She started shaking her head back and forth behind the pillow, then broke down into sobs. Brian had no idea what to do, so he simply wrapped his arms around her and held her while she cried.

They dressed and went upstairs for breakfast. Larry was asleep on the couch in the living room. Brian pointed to him and whispered, "That's my brother. My parents are still asleep." They ate a quiet breakfast of fruity, sugary cereal and fake orange juice. When they were done, Brian followed Jenny to her car.

She opened the door and smiled at him. "Thanks. Don't tell, okay?"

41

Brian didn't know whether she meant her secret, or that they had spent the night together. He decided that neither should be shared. "You bet."

She looked around, then up at the sky. "I wish I didn't, you know, um... have to go. Back, I mean. Home."

Brian shrugged. "You could stay here. Maybe we could figure out what to do about things."

She scratched gravel around with the toe of her shoe. "Your parents..."

He shrugged again. "They don't care what I do. Maybe we can just stay here long enough to find our own place."

"I don't have much stuff. Just, you know... a few sweaters. My jeans. Couple other things."

"Let's go get it. Your stuff, I mean. You shouldn't have to... Go back. To him."

She sniffled. "Will you help me?"

Brian nodded. "Of course. I like you." They hugged. He ran inside, got his keys, and followed her out to the farmhouse.

It was an old, dilapidated looking thing. An eighties-era Ford truck sat in the driveway. She parked next to it, and Brian parked next to her car. When they got out, she said to him, "He's going to get really mad. If he gets his gun, just go away."

"He's got a gun?"

She nodded, and Brian began really considering the ramifications of what he was about to do. He followed her to the front door, and then inside. The house was spotless. An old man, fat, mostly hairless on the head but shaggy everywhere else, and ugly with a red, bulbous nose lay on the couch, snoring. To Brian, the man looked like the stereotypical Creepy Guy. He even wore a white tank top and light blue boxer shorts.

She turned to Brian, put her finger to her lips, and made a shushing gesture. He nodded, and followed her up the stairs. She grabbed a laundry basket from the floor of her plain, small room, and opened a drawer. She threw in all of her clothes: a few sweatshirts, two pair of jeans, another pair of cut offs, some socks, and a few pairs of panties. The only bra she owned was the one she wore every single day.

They crept back down the stairs, but when they reached the bottom, the old man sat up from the couch and turned to look at them. Jenny froze in her tracks, and Brian's heart stopped then leapt to his throat.

"What the hell do you think you're doing?" the old man demanded from across the living room. He smacked his lips together a few times, then looked to Brian. "Get the hell out of my house! Leave Jenny alone!" He waddled over to where they stood, and slapped her across the face. It wasn't a hard slap, it was more like one of those soft slaps that is just meant to get a person's attention. He pointed at her with a dirty, fat finger. "You're in trouble, missy! Do you think he really wants to be with someone like you?"

She clenched her jaw, and looked away from the man. Through her teeth, she said, "Please don't."

He chuckled deep down in his throat, coughed a few times, and turned to Brian. "You don't want her. Get the hell out of here."

Brian shook his head, and turned to Jenny. "Let's go," he said. They started their walk together toward the door again.

The old man's face flushed purple. "You can't take her! She belongs to me! She's crazy! She'll lie!" He turned to Jenny, and yelled, "I never should have let you leave the house. I knew I should have just kept working myself, but *noooooo*! You had to go out and be all grown up. Who needs you anyway?" Sweat beaded on his face and rolled down his neck, soaking into the thin cotton of his undershirt. His color went from purple to a dark scarlet, and Brian thought it sounded like the man was struggling to take in breaths.

Brian and Jenny made their way to the car with the old man following; Jenny opened the passenger door of her Honda, then placed the basket of clothes inside. The old man's face contorted with pain and his right hand reached across his chest and clawed at his left arm pit. He huffed and growled. Brian saw urine soak his boxers, turning them dark blue, then running down his leg.

The old man took a few staggering steps toward Brian, his eyes closed with pain as he wheezed, clutched at his chest, and groaned. The old man fell to his knees, then to his side. His face now looked so dark it was almost black, and his eyes opened then bulged in their sockets. Jenny ran from her car and stood next to Brian. She looked at Brian, panicked. "We have to get help, Brian! Call for help!"

Brian simply shushed her, put an arm around her, and said, "Let him be. I'm glad it hurts him." They watched as the old man suffered. It was a full ten minutes before he died.

In a small town in Iowa, a woman in her early fifties tended to a garden in front of a small white house. A gray tabby cat named Miles trotted along behind her, rolling in the grass when the woman would stop to prune a plant or pick a veggie. In the house, her husband was constructing a ship inside of a bottle, something he had meant to do for years, but only now had gotten around to. Their son gave him the kit for his birthday just a week ago.

The woman heard a car pull up in front of the house, but she paid no attention. Two doors slammed, and she heard footsteps coming toward the house. Visitors. Probably her sister and niece again, in town doing some shopping.

The woman stood and turned to greet her visitors. The first things she saw, and the only things she would remember about that moment for the rest of her life, were the blue eyes of her daughter. It had been seventeen years to the day, and she instantly knew those eyes. She dropped her gardening tools, and as tears streamed down her cheeks, she said over and over again, "Abigail! Abigail!" It became a shout of joy as she repeated the name over and over again. Her husband, making his ship, her son, fixing the sink in the kitchen, and the neighborhoods, tending the gardens in their yards, all heard, and they all knew. Abigail was home.

The Revelation of Pastor Henry

James Christopher walked through the huge, deserted parking lot toward the immense round church building with faux brick siding and a red roof. The steel and glass door opened for him when James pulled on it, and he strolled into the office. The carpet here was dark blue, with short, thick threads. It seemed like it would have been a nice place to walk barefoot.

The church secretary, a plump, middle-aged woman with unnaturally dark hair smiled at him. "You must be Mister Christopher. Pastor Henry is busy just now, but if you wait a few minutes, he'll be right out to see you."

"Thanks." As the woman pushed a button on her phone twice to let the man who ran the church—owned it, really—know that his three o'clock appointment was here, James turned and looked at the welcome sign that stood in the front yard of the church. It read, "Jesus would live a patriotic life." James smiled and softly chuckled at this.

The church secretary noticed his smirk, and asked, "Do you like our sign? I came up with that one myself."

"It's interesting," James replied. "So if Jesus were a patriot, what exactly would that mean?" He glanced down at the etched name plate that stood sentry at the leading edge of her desk. Her name was Jane Anne.

"Well," Jane Anne began, "We'd get out of Israel, that's the first thing. And no more of these liberal agendas."

"So, Jesus would be president?"

"Well he certainly wouldn't be on the Supreme Court!" She giggled at this, as if it was a joke, and had some sort of meaning. James grunted a neutral "Hmph," and scratched his chin, mulling over the different possible meanings Jane Anne may have had.

A minute later, Pastor Henry appeared in the mouth of the hall that led from the waiting area to his private office. He smiled, pointed a finger at James, and said, "I'll bet you're the happy groom!"

James smiled back politely, stood, and said, "Right. Just looking for the right place to get married."

Pastor Henry, his dark hair piled on his head in greased heaps, and his skin a pale white, waved toward the back of the hallway. He was an obese man, and the wave made the loose cup of fat under his chin jiggle. "Well come on back, buddy!" Pastor Henry had a mid-South accent, and the teeth behind his smile were too white and even to be anything but professionally arranged and colored.

James followed the fat man in his suit that was too dark to be called light blue but too light to be called navy blue. It matched the carpet, James noticed, and to fit a fat man so well had to have been the subject of much tailoring. The hallway smelled like the powder that people sometimes pour over their floors before vacuuming. A big whiff might fool anyone into thinking they had just stepped into a fake pine forest made of rubber and vinyl.

When they arrived at the office, Pastor Henry motioned toward a wood and leather chair that sat facing a desk. "Go ahead and take a seat, son." James could tell that Pastor Henry liked calling people "son," because it made him feel superior. James guessed that anything which made Pastor Henry feel superior was on his list of likes.

James Christopher sat down as Pastor Henry parked himself into his chair on the other side of the desk, and James immediately noted that the stiff chair into which he had been placed was closer to the floor than Pastor Henry's was. Anyone coming to visit this place was made to sit in a position that forced them to look upward in order to see their host, and allowed the host to look downward to any visitor.

Pastor Henry was framed by a large bookcase made of some dark, marbled sort of tree. James noted the nice work and clean lines of the carpentry. Every book on the case was either a bible of one sort or another, or a book about the Bible. The only exceptions were a few works by that guy who says that if you pray and are in good graces, God will make you rich. That guy really pissed off James Christopher. On the wall to James's right was a large framed photo of Pastor Henry with his pretty (and much younger) wife, their three kids, and an obese British Shorthair cat curled up at the oldest child's feet.

"James," Pastor Henry began, "You have been a member of our church for about a month, is that right?"

James nodded. "Yes, but my fiancée Terry hasn't joined yet."

"Oh, that shouldn't be a problem. And where is Terry today?"

"Working. Couldn't get the day off, so I'm on my own."

"You came to a place of God. We're never quite on our own here, are we?" Pastor Henry smiled. James smiled back. "I understand that you two are looking for a date in June, is that right?"

"Yes. June twenty-one."

"Okay..." Pastor Henry looked to his computer screen and clicked his mouse a few times. "Okay. Looks like we have the twenty-first open. Great." He turned and looked to James again. "Now tell me, son, when can we schedule a weekend for you and Terry to meet with our young adults pre-marriage counselors?"

"Oh, I hadn't thought of that. What does it involve?"

"It's all about you two discovering where there might be hiccups in the road. You do some testing, talk with other couples who are members of the church and have been married for years."

"It's all weekend?"

"These issues don't work themselves out on their own, son. You and your pretty fiancée are going to need plenty of talking time."

"Sure. How about sometime in May?"

Pastor Henry looked back to his screen. "Yeah, I've got one going the weekend of May 24. Can I put you two down?"

James nodded. He looked around the office some more, and noted more handcrafted furniture. He was interrupted by Pastor Henry. "Okay, I need a check to reserve the chapel for the ceremony, and if you want, you can pay now for your young adults weekend."

"How much for the chapel?"

"Two thousand. The young adults weekend is six hundred. Today I just need half for the chapel, and if you want to wait for a while on the young—"

"Where does it go? The money?"

Pastor Henry scowled at being cut off. "Well, son, the two thousand is for us to open up the church, and to contribute to growing our message in the community. The six hundred does the same."

James looked out the window at the shining Lincoln that Pastor Henry drove to work in. "How much do you make, Pastor?"

A bit irritated, Pastor Henry said "Son, I don't discuss my personal finances. Ministry work is a life commitment."

"That's a nice car out there."

Pastor Henry smiled, and said in a tone he didn't *mean* to be condescending, "Well, son, if you follow the way of the Lord, good things can come to you, too. When you get married, you and Terry do good works, raise a family, and keep your church thriving, and you'll be rewarded in this life as well as the next."

"So poor people are bad, then?"

"No, son. Poor people just have more of the message to get out before their reward comes due. They represent the Lord in the poor areas, where he is needed the most."

"But your car out there—"

"I can't do much for the community if I need to spend my time trying to work a second job to pay for groceries, now, can I?" James was taken aback at how Pastor Henry had snapped at him.

James continued, calmly. "You have a message that God will reward you with good fortune in this life. That those who deserve the good graces of God will become rich."

"I have been blessed, son, with the riches of a wonderful family and the ability to live a comfortable life. When I speak with God at night, he tells me that this blessing is to help me spread his word."

"Your message to the people of your church is the same?"

"Yes."

"And how exactly do people in the community come to God's good graces?" After asking this question, James could see that Pastor Henry was settling down, less on the defensive. Perhaps Pastor Henry believed this young man was only curious.

"The best way to come to grace is to help spread the word of God through the church."

"Coming to church every Sunday?"

"Son, it's about more than just coming to church. You have to be a part of the church. You've been coming here for a month now, and I haven't seen you volunteering with our evangelizing groups. You contribute a bit to the church, but for us to spread our word, we need more of your time and commitment."

"I see. So being blessed with good rewards involves recruiting more church members, and making a strong financial commitment to the church."

"It's all about spreading the word." Pastor Henry smiled.

There was a small pause while the two men smiled at each other. James cleared his throat, and began to reveal what he knew would upset Pastor Henry. "Pastor, I want my marriage to be blessed in the eyes of God. I think it is fair of me to ask you one more thing before committing to doing the ceremony here."

"And what is that, son?"

"It's about my fiancée, Terry."

"Okay."

"Did you know that he's a man?"

Pastor Henry pursed his lips close together, set his jaw forward a bit, and stood from his chair, leaning over the desk and over James. "You're just a troublemaker, aren't you?" His voice was somewhere between a stern lecturing tone and a yell. "The Lord hates homosexuality, it is an abomination. Genesis 18 verse 22!"

"You hate me? Did I do anything to hurt you?"

"Daniel 11 verse 37 tells us that the devil is a homosexual. For all I know, you are the devil himself." Pastor Henry pointed to the door of the office. "Out. Now."

"It's okay with you to yell at me and throw me out? I thought that a church was supposed to be a safe place for anyone who believes." James kept his cool. He could see that the calmer he stayed, the more upset his cool demeanor made Pastor Henry.

"Leviticus 20 verse 13 tells us that homosexuals are to be driven out and killed. I follow the Bible, son, not some liberal agenda the government uses to take away people's true beliefs. Now I think it's best if you get out."

James stood from his chair, and the clothing he wore—a simple tee shirt and jeans—fell away and turned to a long white robe. Pastor Henry yelped as before his eyes, light began to pour from James. When Pastor Henry looked back to James's eyes, a different face looked back at him; a bearded face, with soft, brown eyes and kind features. A face that reflected no notes of hate or fear or anger. It was the face of Jesus himself.

Pastor Henry sunk back into his chair. Jesus smiled. "You know my face now. You have never before known it in your life. You will never know it again, in this life or the next."

"But I spread the word!"

Jesus smiled at Pastor Henry the way an elephant would smile at an ant. "You say you speak to me at night, and that I tell you to spread the word. You lie to the people who come to this church trying to find the truth. You tell them that they can be rich in this life if they are holy, and use yourself as proof. Yet, it is their struggle to find my face that makes you rich, not my good grace."

"I can change."

Jesus slowly shook his head back and forth. "Your destination has been written, Henry. Many of those who you cast from your church will look down from heaven on you as you pass into the gates of hell. You never accepted me as the truth. You used your flock to become rich. For you, passing into heaven will be more difficult than passing your car out there through the eye of a needle."

"I thought it was a camel."

Jesus smiled again. "It once was."

"Why would you tell me you were gay, Jesus?"

"Truly, I say to you, as you did it to one of the least of these my brothers, you did it to me. Every time you encouraged the casting out, the taunting, the bullying; every time, you tore away my robes for the whip. You singled out a group of people to be a focus of evil, and it kept your coffers alive but killed my message.

50

The cross itself could not kill me, but men like you will kill everything I was sacrificed in the name of."

"I can change, Jesus. I..." Pastor Henry's eye rolled back, and he slumped to his chair. He came back to consciousness only a moment later, and watched as James Christopher, the young gay man in jeans a and tee shirt, passed out of his door and down the hall away from his office. Pastor Henry watched out his window as the young man made his way to an old, beat up car and drove out of the parking lot. Pastor Henry knew that he would never see the young man again. As he looked out the window, he saw that the sign in front of the church had been changed. It now read "Too many of those who claim to know me most follow my word the least."

The Good Life

Paul Jacobs took a long, slow drink from his bottle of beer and looked up to the stars. The night was cooling off fast. He closed his eyes, sniffed the atmosphere with a deep, drawn inhalation, and thought to himself that it smelled like rain was coming. When he opened his eyes again, a mist had started to form in the park that comprised the center of the block he lived on.

Every other house around the perimeter of the block was dark. It was almost three in the morning, and nobody else in the neighborhood would be up. He sipped his beer again, and surveyed each house, thinking about who lived in each one, what he knew about them, and how pleased or displeased he was when his kids played with theirs. Every house had practically the same architecture. Paul sighed and said quietly to himself, "Viva la suburbs, buddy."

Because of the way the block was built, a perimeter wall of homes with a park in the center, when Paul looked out from his balcony, he saw the back of every other house. There was the deep blue house on one corner, where an older couple lived. They had a bunch of fruit trees in their back yard, and always let the neighborhood kids pick pears and apples. A few houses down from them were the Russian couple who always seemed to argue over mundane things, like who got to take the nicer car to work the next day. They had a six-year-old girl who liked to come over and play with Katie, even though Katie was a year younger. Nice kid.

The house straight across the park from Paul's place had just been sold. He hadn't met the couple yet, but he heard they were his and Ellen's age, also with a five-year-old and a baby. No idea if the kids were a girl and boy, like his. Paul prided himself on knowing all of his neighbors, and would be one of the first ones to greet them when they showed up with a moving van.

He set his beer on the flat top of the wooden railing, and pulled out the stub for the plane ticket that had brought him home late from his business trip. A week of auditing sales records for the stores in the Dallas region. It was boring, yes, but he didn't really have to travel that much, and on a week like this, when got home late on Thursday night/Friday morning, he could take Friday off without using any vacation time. It was a great way to get a long weekend with his family.

Across the park, a light in the newly sold house flipped on. Paul could barely see across the park now, the fog between the houses had become so thick. He wondered who was over there so late when nobody had moved in yet. Then Paul thought about the Robertson kid in the red house. Fifteen-year-old little punk. He probably broke in to smoke weed or get laid or something.

Paul decided to go over and check things out. The last thing he wanted for whoever bought the house was for them to move into a place that had gotten trashed by a stoned jerkoff the night before. He took another sip of his beer, then walked the steps down to the back yard, which led directly to the park. None of the neighbors had a fenced back yard, and the effect was that the park seemed to begin and end at the houses themselves, making the space look huge and friendly.

He stepped through the grass and into the mist. It was cold and thick. Paul shivered slightly as he passed back out of the other side of the mist, which ended just before the back yard of the house he was heading for. He looked up at the light, which was on the upper floor of the two-story structure. It was the kitchen light. A shadow passed across the room. Paul decided to check the front door first; maybe there was a car or a moving van in the driveway.

As he walked further onto the lawn, he suddenly felt as though he had forgotten something very important. He stopped and turned, looking back at the mist. Where had he come from? His head swam, and Paul sat on the grass, slightly wet with dew. He closed his eyes hard, and tried to remember how he gotten into this back yard. He had no idea where he had come from, but he remembered that he was going to the front door.

Paul stood and rounded the corner of the house, making his way toward the entryway. When he was about ten feet from the front door, it opened, and a tall, beautiful brunette stepped out. She had olive skin and long legs. Her body was incredible, and Paul found himself staring a bit, wondering where he had seen her face before.

She faced him and smiled brightly. "Paul?"

He shook his head slightly, and realized where he recognized her from. Her name was Bridgette. She had gone to college with him years ago. He had a huge crush on her back then, but only ever got as far as saying hello a few times and walking her to her car one snowy day.

"Bridgette," he said, pointing to her. "Bridgette Vasquez. Wow! You look great! I—I can't believe you remember me. If you hadn't said my name..." He trailed off, as she looked at him in a very confused way.

"What are you talking about," she asked.

Paul became suddenly afraid that he had misidentified her, and stammered a bit. She smiled, looked back at the open door to the house, then to him again. She put on a seductive voice and swayed her hips a little extra as she walked to him, saying, "Oh, I get it. The kids are at my mom's place, so you want to be a bad boy, tonight." She was directly in front of him now, and kissed him on the lips, full and wet, her tongue dancing against the tip of his. She reached down to the front of his pants and caressed him as he instinctively put his arms around her waist.

She pulled away from him slightly, took his hands, and said, "I know there's a box of blankets in the house already. Why don't we put a few down on the floor?" She led him inside to the living room and kissed him passionately again. He kissed her back, pushing his hips against her. She whispered into his ear, "I want you so bad. Call me by my maiden name again, that was pretty kinky."

Her maiden name! Paul backed away from her and shook cobwebs out of his head. "Wait, I can't do this! I'm married, Bridgette. Happily."

She smiled in a confused way, and Paul couldn't help but look at her body again from head to toe. She was amazing! "Ummmm, I'm not sure where you're going with this, Sweetheart. Maybe we shouldn't role play right now, and just enjoy our first sex in the new house."

Paul was confused. "Role play? What do you mean?"

Her smiled dropped to a look of irritation. "Look, do you want sex or not? It's after three AM, Baby, and I'm horny, too, but I'm tired. Quit playing around and take off your pants." She smiled again and walked to him. She unbuttoned his pants, and Paul looked out the window to the mist in the park. He remembered where he had come from. She already had his pants partly down and was starting to caress him with her warm hands. If he didn't stop her soon, there would be no stopping.

He backed away quickly, and pulled up and buttoned his pants. He said, "Look, if we're going to be neighbors this has to stop, Bridgette. I'm happy with my family, I can't screw it up. You are *super* hot, but I just can't."

Now she was irritated again. "What the hell is wrong with you, Paul? Are you stressed out or something? Are you having a nervous breakdown?"

"Look, Bridgette," he stammered, "I'm really sorry. I shouldn't have let you kiss me." He felt sweat on his brow. He was so hard inside of his jeans that it hurt. He didn't know what else to say, so he turned and ran out the door, ready to go home.

He could hear Bridgette behind him, yelling, "Paul, you're scaring me, what the hell is wrong?"

He stopped in the middle of the mist, wanting to hide. He breathed heavy, and wondered if it would be wrong to go home and whack off while remembering what Bridgette's body and kisses felt like. A shadow appeared, then approached him. Paul stood still, unsure what to do; who else would be out here?

The shadow stepped close enough for Paul to see the details of a man's face. He was old, and looked somewhere between kind grandfather and strict English teacher. The man wore jeans and a long sleeve button-up shirt that was white with blue stripes. He smiled at Paul. "Hi," the man said.

Paul looked around him, confused. "Hi. I'm Paul." They shook hands. The old man smiled, and Paul saw that his teeth were perfect. His brown eyes fit well with his silver hair.

The old man said, "I don't really have a name, but it's nice to meet you, Paul. Are you a little confused right now?" Paul

56

nodded. "Yeah, that'll happen." The old man chuckled, then looked to the house where Bridgette had been. The old man asked, "Wonder why she didn't follow you?"

"I guess so." Paul shrugged. He was so confused!

"When you ran here, into the mist with me, you ceased to be a part of her life the same way you are when you're on that side of the fog." He jerked his thumb toward Bridgette's house.

"I don't exist?"

"You exist, no matter which side of the mist you're on, Paul," the old man said. "But on the side you were just on, you're Bridgette's husband. On the other side, you and Ellen are married. In here... well, in here is kind of a limbo, I guess you could say."

Paul rubbed his eyes. "Okay, look, dude. You seem nice and everything, but no way. I should never have let her kiss me. My mistake. I would never cheat on Ellen." He waved his hand at the man in a dismissive gesture. "I'm going home."

As Paul turned, the old man grabbed his shoulder, and said, "Wait." A wave of memories shot through Paul so hard and so fast that he almost tumbled to the ground. His life was completely different in these memories.

The first memory was the day he walked Bridgette to her car in college. He smiled at her as she got in. She said, "Thanks for holding my arm. I was really afraid I'd fall."

He swallowed down his nerves, and asked her, "Do you think maybe you'd like to go to a movie or something with me sometime?"

She smiled and said, "I thought you'd never ask, Paul."

The next memory was Bridgette pulling off her dress in his college apartment. They made love on the living room floor, the couch, and Paul's study desk that his father had bought him as a high school graduation gift.

Another memory now. A wedding day. Instead of Ellen next to Paul, it was Bridgette. They danced and drank and he eventually carried her over the threshold of their honeymoon suite door. Then kids. A boy, Alex, and a girl, Karen. Almost the same age as his kids with Ellen. A wonderful life. Just as wonderful and almost a mirror reflection of his life with Ellen.

The old man let go of Paul's shoulder. Paul turned, his eyes wide with wonder. "What was that?"

The old man smiled. Paul thought he looked somewhat similar to Ernest Hemmingway. "It's what could have been. Could *be*, in fact. You have to choose Paul. Which wife, which children? Two lives you could have led. Two possible pasts, two possible futures."

"What does that even mean?"

"It means that you found me at a sweet spot. That spot where you can pick. These opportunities don't come around to often. Once you choose, the memories of the life not chosen will fade quickly."

Paul was dumbfounded, but after the memories... Two versions of his life swam through his head. Ellen. Bridgette. The kids. Since he had memories of being father to both sets he loved them both as a father would. He turned to the old man. "What about my kids?"

The old man's smile faded, and he slowly shook his head. "That's the toughy, Paul. Whichever life you choose, the kids in the other life are gone. Replaced. Well, half-replaced. Your half. The other half, well, that's going to belong to some other guy's genes." The old man looked down at his watch, then back up to Paul. "Time's almost up, Paul. I hate to put you on the spot like this, but..." He shrugged his shoulders.

Paul looked around at the thinning mist. "Who the hell are you?"

The old man held his hands out in front of him as if to say he didn't know. "God. The devil. Fate. Who knows? I am what I am, and I am here to give you a choice. But you have to choose now, Paul."

Paul looked back and forth between the two houses now. He could see each clearly as the last licks of mist melted away. He turned back to the old man, whose image, like the mist, was fading away. The old man yelled, "Quickly, Paul!"

Paul stammered, "I, I... I can't!" The words were out just a second before the mist had cleared. Paul was alone in the park. He looked to the kitchen window of the house where Bridgette had been. It was dark. He ran around to the front of the house, and there was no sign of anyone present. The car that had previously been in the driveway was gone and the door was locked. Paul walked back to his own house and climbed the balcony steps, unsure of what the hell had just happened.

He was thirsty, and looked for a beer bottle he could have swore he left on the top of the railing. There was nothing there. Paul decided that since he had been seeing things just a few minutes ago, the beer must have been his imagination, too. The dining room light just on the other side of the sliding glass door was still on, just as he had left it.

Paul slid the door open and walked inside. The kitchen was to his right, and when Paul walked into the house, he saw a thin, elderly black man leaning into his refrigerator. Paul shook his head, convinced he was still seeing things. The man stood up straight, holding two bottles of beer. He turned around and locked eyes with Paul. For a second, they just stood there staring at each other. Then the old man yelled, "Amanda! Amanda! Get the gun! Intruder!"

Paul looked around the house. The kitchen wasn't the yellow color he and Ellen had painted it last summer. It was a chocolate color with red trim. The stainless steel tea pot wasn't on the stove, but a large, cast iron frying pan was. A younger woman—it had to be this man's daughter—came running up from the lower level of the house. She carried a large bowl of popcorn. When she saw Paul, she yelled "Get the hell out!" The woman ran for the frying pan, and before Paul knew what was going on, she charged him. He turned and ran straight into the glass sliding door.

Paul rebounded off the door and felt the frying pan smack him right between the shoulder blades. He yelled, "Jesus Christ!" slid the door open, and sprinted out of the house. He hurdled the railing, and landed rough on the ground below.

The woman stood on the balcony above, brandishing the pan. "You get the hell out of here, or I'm gonna kill you! I'll come down there!"

Paul stood and half-ran, half-limped away as fast as he could. When he had gotten about two blocks away, he stopped, sat on the curb, and buried his face in his hands. He cried. Paul Jacobs cried harder than he ever had in his life. Harder than when his first cat, a fat Siamese named Daisy, died.

Memories. Three sets now, but two were fading fast. He pulled out his cell phone and wrote a note of everything he remembered. *Ellen. Bridgette.* The date, *May 18* and *3 AM*. He tried to remember his address, but couldn't. He decided to go back to the house where Bridgette had been. He was too afraid of the woman with the frying pan to go to the house that he thought of as his. He noted the address when he got to Bridgette's house, *18746 Broomhill Road, Eagan MN*.

***

Paul sat back on the curb. The two sets of memories were almost gone. He couldn't remember the names of his kids. The strongest memory now was of a new life. He looked at his left hand. No ring. That made sense, because he kept thinking that he lived with a guy named Brad, and went to the bars a lot to troll for chicks.

Paul reached into his pocket, and fished out the ticket stub from his earlier flight. He had still come back from Dallas, so he probably still had the same job. Damn. He pushed his cell phone into that pocket and reached into the opposite pocket.

Wallet and keys. Good. The keys were completely different than the ones he used to carry. He didn't remember how exactly. The key ring had no bauble on it. There was a car key, a fob, and a house key. He jingled them and shoved them back into his pocket. He looked at his wallet. A small single-fold square of leather that held $237 in cash (mostly twenties), two credit cards, a scrap of paper that read "Beth 214-555-3981", and his driver's license.

He looked at the picture on the license. In it, he had a beard (when the hell had he ever had a beard?). He rubbed his face to confirm it was now clean shaven, then looked at his address. Instead of Eagan, he now lived at 620 River Avenue, Unit 2630, in Minneapolis. Paul slowly shook his head back and forth and said to himself, "Holy shit, that's a downtown condo. God, I must be way under water on my mortgage in a place like that."

60

Minneapolis was way too far to walk, so Paul figured his car had to be close. He pulled out his keys and slipped his wallet back into his front pocket. Between the houses, Paul saw a red and blue reflecting light. He turned and saw that across the park a police cruiser was pulling up in front of his old house. The lights turned off, and an officer got out of the car. The slamming door echoed between the houses. Paul said, "Shit," and looked around. No cars parked on the street anywhere. Someone's cat trotted across the quiet street and disappeared under a hedge.

He jogged to his left and looked down the next street. No cars. He wanted to avoid the house he had been thrown out of (it suddenly didn't seem like his house anymore). He couldn't remember what kind of car he drove for the life of him. He jogged back to his right for a few blocks, looking up and down side streets as he went.

When he saw a car, he would hit the unlock button on the fob and see if the lights turned on. On his fourth try, he got lucky. The lights flashed on a car, and he ran to it. When he saw what it was, he pumped his fist and said, "Yeah!" He hit the fob again to confirm he had the right car. The 2009 Mustang unlocked and flashed its lights at him. Paul ran his fingertips across the hood as he went to the driver's door and whispered, "I love you."

He could hear another car slowly making its way down the street. Paul turned, and saw the police cruiser about two blocks down, heading his way. The cop was using his spotlight to look around the neighborhood. Paul jumped into his Mustang, switched off the dome light, and ducked down, waiting. A minute later, the spotlight flashed through the car, lighting the interior up. It stopped there for a second, and Paul held his breath, wondering how he could possibly explain what had caused him to end up in a stranger's house at three in the morning.

The spotlight moved on, leaving Paul huddled on the floor of his car, afraid and shivering. He thought he should wait for a while before starting the car and leaving, in case the cop was watching. Paul pulled out his cell phone again and looked through his games file, deciding to pass the time for a few minutes to catch up on any games he was in the middle of with friends. It seemed like every game he played was against the same Brad person he lived with. He played a turn on a few different games, then sat up and looked around. No sign of the police cruiser. Paul started the car, and drove to Minneapolis. As he went, he began remembering the way to his condo.

Memories kept coming to him. He had totally forgotten whatsherface and that other babe. He shook his head and said, "Wow. Married." He snorted out a laugh, and remembered what he had been doing tonight. When he turned on his phone after his flight landed, a woman named Judy had sent him a text reading "Booty call at my place tonight?"

Paul smelled the collar of his shirt. Perfume. He remembered now. Judy! Yeah, she was a rocket. Red hair, long legs. They'd hook up every few weeks. Mostly a come-and-go type thing. Mmmm. Juuuuudy.

He pulled into the parking garage, and parked in his reserved spot. Paul grabbed his small overnight bag he had travelled to Dallas with, and ran up the first five flights of stairs. He felt great! Paul took the elevator at floor five, only a bit winded from the stairs.

When he opened the door to his apartment, there was Brad. Like almost every night that he wasn't at the bar, Brad was up late playing an online battle game on the huge flat screen TV that hung on the wall. The apartment shook with the sound of a grenade. Paul laughed, "Hey, I'm home! We're going to get another noise complaint if you don't turn that down."

Brad turned and said, "No, dude. What will happen is I'll get my shit blown to hell again if you don't grab a fuckin' controller!" His long, curly brown hair matched the color of his eyes, and he wore cotton gym shorts and a tee shirt. The condo was full of paintings Brad had done. A few nudes (always a good excuse to get a lady naked), but mostly landscapes.

Paul grabbed two beers out of the refrigerator, and handed one to Paul as he sat down and grabbed a controller, entering the game. Brad asked, "How was Dallas?"

Paul shrugged. "Okay. Boring."

"How come you got home so late, dude?"

"Judy texted. Booty call."

Brad laughed. "Dude, you need to cut that shit out or one of these days she's going to lock you in her house and make you her slave or some shit."

***

The next day Brad pounded on Paul's door at noon. "Hey! Are you gonna work out this morning or not?"

Paul sat up, said, "Yeah, fine," and got out of bed.

They walked the treadmills alongside each other. Paul, walking slowly and with a slight limp on his treadmill turned to Brad. "I had the weirdest dream last night. I was married to these two chicks—"

"Mormon love!" Brad shouted to the empty fitness room, throwing his fists in the air.

"No, not like that."

"Hey, what does a Mormon mean if he tells you he's got his own golf course?"

Paul smiled, "What?"

"He's got eighteen wives!" They laughed.

"Okay, so this dream... I was married, but I had like, two lives. I had to pick one." Paul stopped for a second to think. "Hey! I wrote down notes!" He took his phone out of the pocket of his shorts and set it on the console of the treadmill, then navigated to his note from the night before.

"Weird," he said to Brad once he found the note. "Just a couple of names, the date and time, and an address."

"What are the names?"

"Ellen and Bridgette."

Brad smiled, and said, "Three way?"

"No. Quit being disgusting for a minute, I want to figure this out."

Brad was truly offended, and replied, "But you love it when I'm disgusting."

Paul looked at him. "Sorry. It's just that when I look at these names, I feel really different. Like they mean something, or my life would be different somehow if..." He looked back at the

63

names. "You know, I broke up with a really great girl named Ellen right before I moved downtown from my old college apartment."

"Yeah, I remember that when I answered the ad for a roommate you mentioned something about having just broke up with a girl before you bought the condo," Brad said, nodding his head. "So who's Bridgette, then?"

"The only Bridgette I can think of that I've ever even known was this *super* hot chick in college. I think that her parents moved here from Mexico."

"Ever date her?"

Paul shook his head. "No. I almost asked her out once, but chickened out. I had the perfect opportunity, too. I walked her out to her car, because it was snowy, and she was afraid she'd fall down."

Brad guffawed a laugh, and said, "You? Mr. Ladykiller Champion of the twenty-first century? *You* chickened out?"

Paul shrugged. "I never really got the hang of picking up chicks until I had you for a wingman." They high-fived, but Paul suddenly felt very horrible for never settling down. Ellen and Bridgette were important, somehow. He just couldn't remember *why* they were so important.

As Paul was gazing off into space, thinking about Ellen and Bridgette and beginning to wonder what they were up to now, Brad said, "There's more on the note there, buddy."

"Hu?" Paul snapped back to reality. "Oh, yeah. The date and time that... I don't know, that I had the dream, or woke up or whatever, and then the address of the place where... What the hell happened there? It's so weird, Brad. I remember falling asleep while Judy was in the shower, then the next thing I know I'm in some guy's house, and his daughter is chasing me—No, check that, she actually *whacked* me, with a frying pan."

"Holy shit! Really?"

"Yeah, I jumped off of their deck."

"That's why you're limping!"

"Yeah." Paul shook some of the cobwebs out of his head. They walked silently for a few more minutes, until he looked at Brad, and asked "Do you ever wonder what would have happened if you had chosen a different life? Like, if I hadn't talked you into dedicating yourself to your art—"

"So you could watch me paint naked chicks, by the way."

"Well, yeah, but remember when you were just going to give it up and go back to school to be a mechanic? I mean, think about what your life would have been like."

"I could trade lube jobs for blow jobs!"

Paul became irritated, and snapped, "Enough with that stuff! I'm sick of it. If you were a mechanic, how would your life be different?"

Brad shrugged, not wanting to be serious, but giving up his fight to be disgusting. "I guess I'd be pretty unhappy. I mean, I love to paint. I'd rather paint cityscapes and nature scenes than figures, to tell you the truth. But fixing cars... that was just to pay the bills."

"And you're paying the bills pretty well right now with your paintings, aren't you?"

"Well, I don't think I'll ever get rich."

Paul smiled, and said, "Yeah, but you've got me to buy your drinks."

***

Later that day, Paul sat in his room in front of his computer screen, wasting time reading news. He looked at the note on his phone again. Ellen. What was her last name? He remembered really liking her. She was great in bed. Why did he break up with her?

It was some time in the fall, because she wanted to go to an apple orchard on a Saturday. They went, and met her mother there... no, wait. Her mother had just *been* there, with Ellen's younger sister and a cousin about her sister's age. They ran into them as they were sampling different ciders. When they got in the car afterward, they drove silently back toward Ellen's apartment. She sensed what was bothering Paul, and said, "I didn't plan on them being there, Paul. I really like you, yeah, but I don't know if I'm ready for you to meet my parents or anything like that."

"Mmm hmm." He was pissed. There had been a girlfriend or two who had ambushed him with family or a best friend in the past. It was sneaky, manipulative, and rotten. He didn't say

65

another word to her the whole drive back, and she didn't try to talk to him, either. He kept thinking to himself that maybe he should believe her; she'd never lied to him before. She was pretty much everything he had wanted in a woman. She was absolutely beautiful, with long, curly blond hair and bright blue eyes. She was only five-three, but it seemed like four feet of that was curvy, muscular leg.

He pulled up to her apartment, and she said simply, "I'm sorry, Paul. If you think you can believe me that I didn't plan that, then call me again. If not, then you're a jerk anyway for thinking I'd lie to you." He snuck one last peak at her legs as her skirt lifted briefly in the wind when she left the car.

Paul stared at his computer screen. "Ellen Krastner" was typed into the search bar. He hit return, and began tracking her down.

***

It was well after dark on a July night, and Paul was doing more research online. Brad knocked on the door. "Hey, buddy," He said from the other side, "Are you boxing the clown in there?"

Paul laughed. "No. Come on in."

Brad swung the door open and sat on Paul's bed. "You about ready to go? We've got at least four bars to hit tonight, and the ladies from that salon in the IDS building have their lawn bowling league at *Barn's*."

Paul leaned back in his chair and cracked his back. "Yeah, they always look so good."

Brad looked longingly to the ceiling and added, "And they always get so drunk."

"Eventually they'll figure out that we're just picking them up one by one until we've been with them all."

Brad shrugged. "I can live with that. Whatcha doin' there?"

"Huh? Oh, this. Yeah..." Paul looked down at a notebook he had next to his computer. It was full of research on Ellen and Bridgette. "Nothing." He flipped the notebook closed.

By the end of the August, Brad was worried. Paul had been spending practically every free hour alone in his room. Brad slipped into Paul's room while he was in the shower and opened the notebook that Paul kept on his desk. On the first page, a line was drawn down the center of the paper. At the top of the left side, Paul had written "Ellen" and at the top of the right side he had written "Bridgette". Underneath, he had, side by side, noted their height, weight, birth dates, their parents' names, and where they had gone to high school.

Brad flipped to the next page. Two columns again. This time, past and present home addresses. Page three was filled with Facebook friends and phone numbers. Page four, work information. Brad kept flipping through the notebook, and realized there were at least twenty pages like this. Paul's voice behind him made him jump. Paul asked, "What are you doing in my room, Brad?"

His voice was calm. Brad turned around and said, "Jesus, dude. Don't talk so calm. You should be pissed at me."

Paul did his best impression of the computer on *2001: A Space Odyssey* and said, "I afraid can't do that, Brad."

"Cut it out, man. You know that movie freaks me out."

Paul smiled. "Fine. Just erase your internet history off my computer, I don't want to know what you were doing on there."

Brad held up the notebook. "What are *you* doing on there, Paul? This is some serious stalker shit."

"If I wanted to live with someone who digs through my stuff, I would have moved in with a woman."

"Yeah," Brad said, "Well, not to sound too girly or anything, but this is pretty scary stuff. I mean, you were telling me about that dream you had a few months ago and now this. What the hell is going on with you?"

"I don't know." Paul sat on the bed and leaned forward, cupping his forehead in his palms. "I'm so confused. I just... I feel like I missed something. Like I need to go back and make something right."

"You didn't, like, boil their rabbits or anything, did you?"

"No, you asshole!" They looked at each other, and started laughing. Paul said, "I guess it *is* kind of weird, huh?"

"Yeah, it's weird. So now that you've got all this information, what are you going to do?"

Paul shook his head. "I don't know. Ellen is married to some guy named Rick Carlson—"

"Sounds like an asshole."

"Yeah, he kind of does. He runs a used car lot. They have three kids."

"Okay, so what about Bridgette?"

"She's married, too. Two kids. She's some kind of secretary."

Brad furled his brow and stuck his finger out at Paul. "Hey, they're administrative assistants! They work hard. Secretaries just get coffee for people."

"Whoa, settle down, Margaret Sanger."

"My mom is an administrative assistant."

"Okay. You are Brad, hear you roar."

"That's enough."

They sat silently, staring at each other for a few moments. Paul said, "I want to go see each of them. See how they're doing. If they have a good life. Do you want to come along?"

Brad thought about it for a second, then asked, "Can we go to the bar and pick up random whores afterward?"

"Sure."

Brad smiled. "Good! Because ever since this whole Ellen and Bridgette thing, you've sucked as a wingman."

***

Bridgette's house was modest, but kept up well. They pulled up across the street and parked. It was late afternoon, and the streets were empty of the kids who were home for supper. The houses in the neighborhood were small and close to each other. Paul said, "We'll have to go around into the back yards."

"What, why?"

"Because, I need to see inside."

"I'm pretty sure that's not legal, man."

Paul looked at Brad, irritated. "What did you think I came here to do? Inspect her mail box?"

Brad giggled and said, "Only if she's got her bedroom window open."

Paul laughed. "Anyway, I'm going to see what I can see. Are you coming, or are you going to sit in the car?"

"Tell you what," Brad replied, "I'll sit in the car. That way, if you get arrested, I can bail you out."

"Fine. Text me if you see cops coming. I think they're still looking for me after the whole frying pan thing, anyway."

"Okay. Whoa, wait. The cops are looking for you?"

"They showed up that night and cruised the neighborhood, but they probably forgot all about it since then. Besides, that was in Eagan. We're in Brooklyn Heights now; cops in different suburbs probably don't even talk to each other."

As Paul was getting out of the car, a slightly panicking Brad said, "Cops talk, Paul. Cops talk!" He watched Paul jog across the street and duck into a back yard near Bridgette's house. "My best friend is a fuckin' felon. I need to take notes for a memoir."

The back yard was empty and quiet, and Paul decided that if he stayed low and in the middle of as much vegetation as possible, the people in the house probably wouldn't notice him. As long as he didn't make himself conspicuous, and everyone stayed inside, he figured it was safe to look into the windows from a distance.

The house was decorated for a party. A banner made of paper letters painted in bright, metallic tones of color and reading "HAPPY BIRTHDAY" hung over the wide opening between the living room and dining room. The house was nice inside; clean, painted in bright colors. A man, handsome, but graying early, walked out of the kitchen carrying plates. A little girl carrying silverware followed him. She was in turn followed by a very little boy, who tottled around after his big sister in adoration. Paul smiled to himself, and thought *This is a happy home.*

Paul looked over to the couch, where a long, thin greyhound lazed, watching the family. His head raised up and looked at the front door at the same time Paul registered the sound of a car pulling into the driveway. The engine stopped, and a door opened, then slammed. Paul held his breath and watched the front door, which led into the living room.

The door swung open, and there she was, as beautiful as he remembered her. Bridgette wore a business suit that showed off her figure. The blue skirt hugged her legs the way Paul suddenly longed to. She set down her purse on a table beside the doorway as the man and daughter rushed in from the dining room and shouted "Happy birthday!" They were followed by the tottler, who ran behind them with his hands straight up in the air, yelling "Dot dot dot dot dot!"

Bridgette laughed, and it made her look even more beautiful. Paul's jaw dropped slightly when she bent down to hug her children and he could see how her legs led to the gracious, beautiful curves of her bottom. She stood and leaned to her husband. They gave each other a long kiss, and Paul imagined the way her lips must feel. It was almost as if in some other time, in some other place, he had kissed those lips rather than just dreaming about it after class so long ago.

She was happy. She had a wonderful family. Paul could easily picture himself in the shoes of her husband. He wanted to just sit in the back yard and watch her all night, but decided that he had to come back to reality. It was obvious that Bridgette had the perfect life; he had nothing but selfish reasons to want to change anything about it. He returned to the car.

When Paul slipped into the passenger seat, he looked over at Brad. Brad shook his head slowly. "Holy shit, dude," Brad said, "When I saw her get out of that car, I almost got out of this one, ran up to her, and proposed on the spot."

Paul smiled. "Yeah, she looks good."

Brad shook his head faster, and said, "It's more than just that. I mean, I don't know what it is, but that chick is *perfect*! We have to go home, I need to paint her."

***

Paul was on his own the next two nights, as Brad dove fully into painting Bridgette. When he was finished, the portrait was incredible. Paul looked at it quietly as the last touches of paint dried. There she was, standing nude beside a fountain. The area around the fountain was cobblestoned, and a stucco wall with arched windows rose behind her. She stood at such an angle that the front of her body was fully visible, yet she was turned just a bit so that the curve of her left cheek was also shown above her long, muscular legs. She looked into the lowest pool of the fountain, which had three smaller pools above it with water cascading down. The higher pools all had wonderful birds bathing and singing to her. Her right hand was up to her face, the middle three fingers gently touching the corner of her mouth. Her left hand reached tentatively toward the fountain.

Paul sighed, "Wow, Brad. This might be the best thing you've ever painted."

Brad looked at the painting; to Paul, it seemed almost as if he looked *through* the painting. He said, "I'm the fountain. She looks at me and sees a different reflection of herself. The red birds are our children, with me giving them food and shelter, and her giving them love and life. The blue birds are the challenges of life, held within the grasp of my pools so that she never has to worry. The yellow birds are our friends. They play and bathe in me, the fountain, but stand in awe and adoration of Bridgette's beauty."

Paul whistled through his teeth, and said "I thought *I* had a crush on her."

Brad stretched his shoulders so that his back cracked, then scratched his chin. "I need a drink."

Paul nodded. "Sure. And dinner."

***

The waitress took their plates when the burgers were finished, and each man stared at his nearly-empty glass of beer. Brad said quietly, "So after seeing Bridgette..."

"Yeah," Paul said, "I totally need to check out Ellen."

Brad slapped his hand down on the table. "It's a mission!"

It was a long drive to Ellen's house, and when they got there it was well past dark. They crept together through the back lawns of the neighborhood, using Paul's phone to navigate through the huge yards. They found Ellen's house near a pond. The house loomed on a lot that was separated by the other large homes in the neighborhood by thick rows of trees. Ellen's dark brown house

71

was big—used car dealer big. Paul said, "Wow, this guy must really be loaded."

They climbed trees to see inside. The first room they saw was the living room, where Ellen sat with all three kids watching a cartoon movie. She looked pretty, but Paul thought she looked somehow sad in the exact opposite way Bridgette had looked happy. Her eyes lied about her age, and combined with the first few frown lines around her mouth, made her look about ten years older than she was.

Paul and Brad could see around the corner of the house, and they watched as a shiny SUV pulled into the garage. In the living room, Ellen leaned over to each child one-by-one and kissed the tops of their heads. Nobody got up to greet the man who appeared in the living room a few minutes later.

When he said something to the group, Ellen stood and walked out of the room. Her husband followed, and the light in the next room, the dining room, turned on. The windows were closed, so Paul and Brad couldn't hear the conversation, but the exaggerated hand gestures, angry faces, and pointed fingers mimed a fight between Ellen and her husband. She shoved him and yelled at him. The kids turned from the TV and looked in the direction of the living room, then back to their movie.

Ellen stormed off out of view. A few seconds later, a light on the lower level turned on. Paul scrambled out of the tree. Brad followed, asking, "What are you doing?"

"I want to get a closer look."

As they trotted toward the window, Brad said, "They'll see us if we get too close."

Paul shook his head, and said, "No. If the light inside is on, they can't see very far out into the dark."

"How do you know that?"

"I used to do a lot of toilet papering in high school."

Brad giggled, and followed Paul closer to the window. It was a large, beautifully adorned bedroom. Ellen had already opened a suitcase, and was throwing in handfuls of her husband's clothes. He entered the room, and yelled at her. Paul and Brad could now hear the couple well enough to make out what they said.

The husband yelled, "At least she gives me what I want! You don't even care!"

Ellen turned from the suitcase to face him. She was crying now. "I don't care? Really, Rick? I don't care? Those are our kids up there!" She pointed upward, toward the living room where the children watched TV. "I've put up with the cocaine, the lying about money, looking the other way while you rip people off and get bogus loans from the car companies, all because I thought it was best for them. I care, Rick. I care about our kids. And if you cared about them, too, you'd quit screwing that no-good whore and start to act like a real man!"

Brad whispered to Paul, "Rick! I had forgotten what his name was."

"Shh!"

Rick stormed over to Ellen, and grabbed her mouth with his hand, and pushed her against the wall. She was obviously in pain as he clutched her, squeezing the flesh on her face so hard that his forearm shook. "You don't think I'm a man, huh? You don't think I'm a man!" He let go of her jaw, wound back his hand, and slapped her across the face hard enough that Paul and Brad heard the *smack!* through the window as Ellen fell to her knees. Paul began a motion to run around to the front of the house, and Brad instantly grabbed him around the shoulders and held him back, saying, "You don't want to do that, buddy. Nothing good can come of it."

Paul looked at Brad pleadingly. Brad shook his head. Paul knew he was right. If he rushed into the house, things would only get much, much worse. They looked back to the window. Ellen was now laying face-down on the bed, sobbing. Rick was finishing packing his bag. He turned to her, and, jabbing his finger into the back of her head with every word, shouted, "You're not getting a fucking *dollar* out of me!"

He stormed off. After a moment, they heard the garage door open, the SUV pull out, then screech its tires and drive away fast. Ellen just lay on the bed and cried, until all three kids came down after a couple of minutes and piled around her, hugging her and cuddling into her sides.

Brad nudged Paul. "We should go, man.

"Yeah. You're right."

***

The apartment was quiet. Brad painted, Paul read. It had been months since the visit to Ellen. Paul flipped the page over and sighed. Chapter break. He closed the book, set it down, and walked over to the refrigerator. "Hey Brad, need a beer?"

"Does it burn when a porn star pees? *Yes*, I need a beer!"

As Paul walked into the living room, which was also serving as Brad's studio, he asked, "Whatcha painting tonight?"

"Oh, still working on the view of the lake from my parents' cabin."

"Got some time for a video game? It's been a while since we've conquered any college stoners who dare to get online and challenge us."

"Sure." They turned on the TV and game console, then sat next to each other on the couch. As the game started, Brad said, "The Jackson Street Gallery called about my portrait of Bridgette."

"Yeah?"

"Yeah. They want it for their permanent collection."

Paul smiled, and said, "Nice!"

"Do you ever think about her and Ellen anymore?" Brad asked.

Paul shrugged. "Yeah. In a couple weeks it'll be May 18 again."

Brad sipped his beer and asked, "Think it means anything?"

"I don't know. I wake up in the middle of the night thinking about it, though. Like I should do something."

"I wake up in the middle of the night to pee."

Paul laughed, "What the hell does that have to do with anything?"

Brad smiled and said, "I don't know, I just wanted to have some reason to wake up, too."

***

May eighteen. It fell on a Friday this year. Paul left work late and had dinner alone. He left the restaurant and went to a bar

74

to have a couple of beers. The baseball game was on, and he watched until it was finished at ten. His text alert sounded; it was Brad: *Hey, buddy. Met some honeys. Come to Manny's.*

Paul sighed. Why not hang out? Maybe hooking up with a bar whore would take his mind off of things. He paid his tab, and jumped in his Mustang.

Manny's, a small dive bar, was loud with voices. Paul worked his way through the crowd and found Brad in the middle of a bachelorette party. A completely drunk blond hung off of him. She was a little thick in the middle, but not bad. If she were sober and not draped around Brad's neck like a Hawaiian lei, she might even be cute. Brad looked to Paul and shouted, "Heeeey!"

They bumped fists, and Paul ordered a round for the table. In a few minutes, a short brunette from the group was talking with him. He went to her house with her after closing time. The sex was mediocre. She was pretty loaded, and more or less laid quietly on the couch while Paul tried to enjoy her body as much as he could. He kept checking his watch, but she didn't seem to care.

Afterward, Paul got dressed and checked his watch again. "Hey, Janet, I have to run."

She lay naked on the couch, half asleep. "It's Julie. Call me sometime, alright?"

"Sure." He stood and walked out, deleting her number from his phone on the way to his car. It was after two. Paul took a few deep breaths of fresh, cool air to get his head straight, then sat in the driver's seat and started the engine.

He popped open his phone, and typed in the address from his note. If he drove fast, he could make it there around 2:45 and have time to think about what the hell it was that he wanted to do when he got there. Certainly not get whacked with a frying pan again.

***

He parked outside the address and sat quietly. It was just before three. Paul decided to get out and walk around for a bit. His head was swimming, and he knew he shouldn't have been driving. He never would have come out here if he had been sober. Or would he?

75

He remembered that the block was built in a unique manner, with the central area a large grassy park in the middle of the houses. He decided to go there and just sit on the grass and try to sober up a bit. He kept thinking to himself that he shouldn't have come to this place. The father and daughter he felt guilty about scaring the hell out of would probably see him and call the cops, or worse yet chase after him.

He crept into the park. No lights on anywhere. Paul sat on the grass in the middle of the park and looked up at the stars. They pinwheeled over him slowly. He closed his eyes and got a bit dizzy, so he let himself tumble over onto his side. He must have fallen asleep, because the next thing he knew, a hand gently shook him. "You okay?" a male voice asked.

Paul looked up, and saw Brad standing over him. He stood, and noticed that there was dew on his clothes—he had been asleep for some time. "What are you doing here, Brad?"

"The sun will be up soon. You never came home... I got nervous and remembered you telling me about that crazy night a year ago. You had the address of that house across the way written down on your notepad. I decided to come out and look for you."

A light haze hung in the grass as a chill set in. Paul sat on the grass again and huffed out a sigh. Brad sat next to him. Shaking his head, Paul said, "I remember it, Brad. I remember what happened. I was married to Ellen. I walked over here, and there was this fog."

Brad nodded. "Yeah, it looks like the grassy area lies a little low."

"It does," Paul replied. "When there's a big rain, and in the spring when the snow is melting, the water pools up here and the kids play in it."

"So what do you remember, man?"

"Well, like I said, I was married to Ellen. I walked over to that house, over there," he pointed to the house where Bridgette had been, "And when I got there, I was married to Bridgette. We made out, and I took off for home."

"Wow, scary hot girl chased you away, huh?"

"Not funny."

Brad shrugged. "Sorry."

"So anyway, when I got back to the grass, there was some old guy in the fog. He told me I had to choose which life I wanted."

"If you had to choose between Ellen and Bridgette, how'd you end up with me?"

"I didn't pick fast enough."

"Huh." They sat silently for a minute, then Brad said, "Want to hear something funny?"

"Sure."

"I don't know if it's your crazy story or what, but I think I know what that house you went into looks like on the inside."

Paul looked over at the house that Bridgette had been moving into. "What do you mean?"

"I mean there's an oh-eight Silverado in the garage. A pool table in the basement. The three kids sleeping in the downstairs bedrooms are named Charity, Ben, and Mickey. The dining room table has a big scratch in it from one of Mickey's toys. A big mutt of a dog named..." he thought for a second, "Named Jimbo is asleep on the foot of the bed in the master suite."

Paul punched Brad in the shoulder. "You're such an asshole! I open up and tell you about this stuff I'm going through, and you start making up shit. You're a jerk."

Brad steeled his eyes at Paul and shook his head. "No, man, I'm not. I think I have the key to that house in my pocket."

They were startled when a voice said, "You do." The haze around them had grown into a fog, and the old man that Paul had seen a year earlier walked through it. He sat in front of the two friends.

Brad pointed to the old man and asked Paul, "This your dude?" Paul nodded, and Brad looked at the old man. "Why do I remember things that never happened, man? This is kind of freaky."

The old man asked, "Which life made you happy?"

Paul and Brad looked at each other, not knowing who he spoke to. The old man said, "Paul, you go first."

Paul shrugged. "They were all good. In two lives, I had a wonderful wife and kids. In the third, I had a lot of fun living with my best friend. I was happy no matter what."

The old man turned to Brad. "And you?"

Brad smiled. "I still paint in both. I don't mind being a mechanic. At least I can pay the bills." He turned to Paul and said, "Maybe you have a tough time deciding, buddy. I don't. My wife is in bed. I'm going to crawl in next to her. Maybe I'll see you around." He stood and began to walk away, then turned and said, "We had another dog, you know. She died, right out there on that street. A car hit her, just a couple days ago. Paul, no matter what you choose, there is life and death, good and bad. You have to choose your life and you have to be happy with it. I mean, really, truly happy through everything that happens. You've been a good friend, but I can't go back that way. Good luck, buddy." Brad turned and walked away, the mist enveloping him so he faded from sight like a ghost.

Paul turned to the old man. The set of memories he wanted lay at the front of his mind. He pushed everything else away. "I'm ready."

"Ellen?"

"Yeah."

"And you know..."

"Yes, I know how hard things are right now. I have all the memories of the last year with Ellen. It's that life I choose, and I have to accept that every other life is never going to be. I want to be with her in the end."

"For every choice," the old man said, "An infinite number of other realities disappear. You could have chosen any life you wanted, Paul. I admire your love for her."

In the morning, when Ellen woke, Paul was sleeping tight against her. She slipped out from beneath his arm and slid open the dresser drawer. The forest of pill bottles inside loomed. Paul awoke and shifted to sit next to her on the bed.

She tried to speak, but only croaked out a sound, so she cleared her throat and said, "I've only got a few more months, Paul. Do I really need to keep taking all these?"

He leaned over and kissed her bald head, missing the lovely hair that had once grown there. "If you don't want to, you don't have to, honey. How do you feel today?"

A tear ran down her eye. These past few weeks, knowing that the end was so near, had been so hard on her. Paul had been so good to her, had been everything she could have wished for. "I feel like it isn't fair that I'm going to leave you alone to raise our kids. I feel like, if I could, I'd give you a whole other life to live, where you wouldn't wake up next to a dying woman every morning and have to be so strong."

He kissed her head again, and said, "I wouldn't want any life that didn't have you in it."

Sirens' Fade

The slow, heavily orchestrated waltz cut off so fast that Bob and Helen Murray just kept dancing for a few steps in their silent living room. A cranky, electronic series of tones blasted out of the radio's speakers, followed by a high-pitched squeal. Bob instinctively reached up for his hearing aid, and Helen pulled his hand back down to his side.

A moment later a man's voice, too perfect to be anything but pre-recorded, came through the speakers, announcing "This is the emergency broadcast system. A nuclear attack is imminent for your area. Citizens are advised to take shelter immediately in a basement, storm shelter, or low-lying area. This is not a test. Do not go outside. Seek shelter immediately. If you are outdoors and away from shelter, find a low-lying area, such as a ditch or pit. Do not take shelter in a vehicle. Proceed immediately..."

"Bob, what's happening?" Helen looked to her husband with large, frightened eyes. He hadn't seen that look in her eyes since the emergency room, so many years before, when their son lay bleeding on a bed waiting for surgery. Bob clicked off the radio and pushed the power switch on the old television the couple had received decades ago as a wedding gift. The screen showed an empty office with an American flag behind a large wooden desk, and the voice that accompanied the picture was that of the regular evening news anchor, in the middle of a statement. "...where this attack has originated. The White House has told us that within a few minutes, a spokesperson for the president will issue a statement. The location of the president has not been released. In the meantime, citizens are advised to take shelter in their basement if they have one. For people without a basement, go to a storm shelter or low-lying area." A ticker ran across the bottom of the screen with the same message repeating over and over: *A nuclear strike has begun against the United States. All citizens are advised to immediately take shelter. If you hear a nuclear blast, do not look at it.* Now the first long, sorrowful whine of the emergency sirens began.

There was no TV or radio in Jacob's bedroom. He lay between his parents, enjoying his first grown-up bed, while they read him a chapter out of *The Last Battle* by C.S. Lewis. The nine year-old boy was just beginning to drift off when the howl of the siren, on a pole in the park just across the street, began. He sat up and looked at his dad. "Is it a tornado?"

The boy's father, a one-armed man named Jim, shook his head. "I doubt it, buddy. It's been pretty calm out there all day." Jim looked to his wife. "You keep reading, Jenna. I'll quick jump online and make sure we don't have a thunderstorm out there wandering around."

She smiled and responded with a quick "'Kay," and went back to the book, doing a different voice for each of the characters. Jim padded out to his office and opened the laptop computer. He smiled when he saw that it was open to a webpage dedicated to zombie shooting games, and reminded himself to scold Jake later. He couldn't be too upset though, since he relied on Jacob's "clandestine" game playing to find out the best games to keep himself entertained while taking a break from his own work. Jim typed in the address for the local TV station that had the best weather reports—OK, the one with the best looking weather girl—and immediately stuck a finger from his lonely left hand into his mouth and bit down.

Tears welled in his eyes and began running down his cheeks as he bit harder and harder, wishing that what he saw wasn't true. He stood, turned, and ran down the hall. Behind him, the laptop's screen had the same image Bob and Helen had seen on their TV screen of the empty office. A flashing announcement of bold black print over a yellow banner read "United States target of massive nuclear attack. Citizens advised to take shelter immediately."

***

Alongside a thin strip of highway outside of Phoenix, a raucous bar crowd sat stunned. Fourteen big-screen televisions all showed the same image: The Diamondbacks star pitcher, a rookie who had just thrown six perfect innings, lay writhing in pain in front of the mound. A tattooed man in about sixteen layers of leather stepped out of the bathroom. "What's going on?"

The bartender, a beautiful young woman who never told any of the patrons her real name, turned and said, "Meyer just took a line drive to the throat."

The mountain of leather, tattoos, and greasy hair reached up to the jagged scar that lay just above the point where his left clavicle met his breast bone, swallowed hard, and said, "Whoa. That's gotta hurt." All at once, the screens in the bar flashed over to the empty office. The tattooed man decided to take a smoke break outside; maybe the network decided that showing an injured man writhe in pain was bad TV, so they decided to cut to something else for a few minutes. When he opened the door, the sound hit him. He couldn't be sure of what it was, but thought maybe it was those damn sirens that kept scaring him every day at noon when he was a kid.

***

Helen flipped her phone closed, and looked to Bob. "Nothing again." Bob grunted, and said "I'm sure all the phone lines are so busy that nobody can get through to anyone. Did you try to send a text?"

Helen shook her head, then nodded, then buried her face in her hands and sobbed. Bob wrapped his arms around her and cooed at her. They swayed back and forth a bit, almost mimicking the dance they had been having together just minutes ago. "He's a smart boy. He'll be fine."

Through her tears, Helen worked out the words "What do we do, Bob? You were in the service. What did they tell you?"

He shook his head. "I was in a place where there was no hope of surviving a nuclear attack. They always told us to just pray it was over quick." He held her tight again. She felt the protection of his body. The love that his strong arms, powerful even now at his advanced age, had always given her. She remembered the way he had held her after the first time they made love; the way he had held her in the hospital while she was so afraid of their son dying.

She looked up at him with wet eyes and sniffed. "This is the end." Bob recognized it as a statement, not a question, and he nodded. She blushed a bit, and quietly asked, "How long ago did you take your pill?"

He scowled at her. "Helen. At a time like this?"

She shrugged. "Call me a goose, Bob, but it's how I want to die. I think it was meant to be that way, otherwise why would we have planned on getting between the sheets tonight?"

He leaned forward, kissed her forehead, and chuckled. "We plan it for every Saturday night, my love."

She pushed herself into his arms, his chest, his warmth, and whispered, "It's what I want." She took his hand in hers, and led him up the stairs to their bedroom.

***

Jim, Jenna, and Jacob sat huddled under the stairs in their basement. A pet carrier next to them held a scared gray tabby cat named Ghost. The radio kept replaying the same messages over and over. Imminent attack. Take shelter. Don't look at the blast. Finally, Jim had enough. He clicked the radio off, and turned to his son. "Jacob, how come you never asked me why I only have one arm?"

The boy, not quite comprehending the gravity of what was going on in the world around him, shrugged. He sat in Jenna's lap, and she squeezed him tight against her, unable to protect him or offer him any defense. She simply stared blankly ahead, wrapped in a blanket of shock. "I guess I always knew. You were a little boy helping your grandpa cut down a tree. You wrapped a rope around your arm to try and hold a branch from coming down, but it was so heavy it tore your arm right off when your grandpa cut it."

Jim nodded. "That's right. How did you know that? I never told you."

"Grandma did. She's told me about it a lot of times. Did it hurt?"

Jim nodded again. "It scared me a lot, too. I thought I was going to die."

"But you were okay. I mean, you know, except your arm."

"Yeah." Jim chuckled. "It got stuck in the tree."

84

Jenna, almost comatose, turned to Jim. In a faraway voice, she said, "Why would you talk about this right now?" Without really wanting an answer, she turned her head back and leaned it against the wall. Jim leaned over and kissed her cheek, then the top of Jacob's head.

"Jake," he said, "I want you to know everything about me that you ever could."

***

In the desert outside Phoenix, the tattooed man was about to turn and go back into the bar when the pretty bartender ran outside and began looking to the sky. She was followed by a stream of patrons, who began scattering to their cars or running down the street. He turned to the bartender and asked, "What's going on?"

She looked down from the sky at him, her face pale and full of fear. "We're under some kind of attack. They say we're getting nuked!" Behind her, a drunken man stumbled out of the bar, yelling "Fuckin' jihad bastards got nukes, dude!" The drunken man stumbled again, and began weaving down the street yelling things about Russians and al Qaeda.

The tattooed man grabbed the bartender by the shoulders, and said in a commanding tone, "Hey. Do you live around here?"

She pointed to her right, and said "A few blocks that way."

"Okay. Let's go." They ran together under the unsurrendering wail of the sirens, and she led him inside of an old brick apartment building that smelled of mildewed wall paper. They went down a set of stairs to the front door of her garden-level apartment. She let the man in, and once they were in her living room, realized that she had just brought in a stranger; a man with long, greasy hair, a nasty scar by his neck, and lots of tattoos. She backed away from him, afraid of what he might do now that the end of world was coming. "Who are you," she asked, trying to mask the fear in her voice.

The man reached inside his thick jacket and pulled out a wallet. He flipped it open to reveal a bright silver badge under a government identification card. "D.E.A. I use your bar as a hot spot to monitor the local biker gangs." He smiled. "I'm not bad, I only look like it." She smiled back, and for a moment he forgot all about

85

the high-pitched warning outside. Coming back to reality, he quickly said, "We need to get under a mattress in your bathtub. Nothing weird, I promise. It's just the best way to take shelter without a basement."

"They train you for nukes in the D.E.A.?"

"No. I grew up in Nebraska. Lots of tornadoes there."

***

In their quiet bedroom, the place where they had made love together for almost their entire married lives, Helen lay naked, curled up to Bob's side, amazed that even at his age, even though he needed a little blue pill to help him out, he could still make love to her in a way that made her feel like she was twenty again. She gently rubbed his chest. "He'll be alright, won't he?"

"Yeah. He knows what to do, Helen. If anyone can make it, it will be him. He's made it through so much already."

"Thank you for making love to me, Bob. For every time in my whole life. You've been a perfect husband all these years."

She saw him smile in the dark. That smile always made him look so handsome. "All I ever wanted was to be a good husband to you."

"You were always a good father, too." She kissed his cheek, and pressed her body closer to his.

***

Under the stairs, Jim and Jacob talked, while Jenna continued to stare ahead blankly, her head against the wall. Jim was in the middle of a story about his days as a kicker on a division three college football team. "They never saw it coming. I mean, who would have thought that this guy—not just a kicker, but a *one-armed* kicker—would take a direct snap and throw the ball instead of going for the field goal." Jake smiled at his dad. Until this moment, Jim never realized how much he wanted to be the little boy's hero.

They were silent for a moment, listening to the sirens. Jacob looked into Jim's face. "Dad, will there be zombies?"

Jim's first thought was to smile and chuckle at the boy, but he realized soon enough to stop himself that the boy was at a

86

complete loss to try and explain what was happening. He ruffled the boy's hair. "No, son. No zombies."

Jenna finally seemed to wake from her funk. She turned to face Jim and said, "What do you think *will* happen, Jim?"

Jim swallowed hard and looked at his hand. He thought about the nights cursing the accident, wishing they could have reattached his arm. Cursing his grandfather, cursing his mother for bringing him there to visit. Now, how many wasted, useless moments those thoughts seemed. Even if he had two hands, no matter how strong they might have been, he was unable to do a single thing to protect his family. He looked to their frightened faces. "What happens next," he said, "Is something that very few people in the world can explain. So really, I don't know. Just remember that no matter what, I love you both with all my heart. If we get separated, let's meet in the front yard. If we can't meet there, let's meet at the pole in the park across the street. Okay?" He was silent for a minute. "Hey, Jacob. Did you know that the book we're reading to you was given to me by my dad when I was in the hospital after losing my arm?"

Jenna sat up straight, and said, "Oh, hey! I brought it. Should we finish it while we're down here? We're on the last chapter."

***

It was dark under the mattress. The bartender sat quietly, trying to think of what to say to this strange protector beside her. "So," she began, "Do you really think we're in danger here? I mean, come on, we're a crappy little town two hours away from Phoenix. Most *Americans* don't even know we exist, let alone give a crap. I doubt if China or Russia or whoever the hell is bombing us knows we're here. Or cares."

The tattooed man grunted out a "Hmph," sighed, and said "I'm pretty sure this part of the country is dotted with a lot of missile silos. Whoever is doing this won't want us to hit them back. We're likely to get hit before a lot of big cities."

"That sucks." She was silent again for a second, then decided to change the subject. "So what's that scar? You get stabbed during a drug bust or something?"

The tattooed man laughed. "No. That happened when I was a kid. I was playing at a neighbor's house, running around with a knife. I tripped on a shoe that one of us left laying on the floor, fell wrong, and ended up spraying blood all over the house. I nearly died. Then when I didn't, I thought my parents were going to kill me. They were so mad."

"Holy shit. Mister responsible undercover government badass was the kid who ran with scissors!" They both laughed.

***

In the end, these seven were some of the lucky ones, the ones who the survivors envied for the few short weeks it took for the human race to wisp out of existence. Those lucky ones who were nothing more than ash, shadows, and bits of bone in the end. They died together, making love, telling stories, becoming friends. Those lucky ones who never saw a flash, never heard a boom. Those lucky ones who died in their beds, or in their homes, or laughing together. In the end the thing they knew was not fear, nor anger, nor pity. In the end, all they knew was the sirens' fade.

Father McKenzie's Kitchen

The tiny concrete block building that the bums all called Father McKenzie's Kitchen sat so hidden that practically the only way to find it was to lose your family, lose your money, lose your home, lose your mind, then move under the large rail bridge and parking structures that sit where the squatters used to set up camp in Lowertown along the Mississippi River in St. Paul. A whitish building with a nicely-tended garden on the side and a junk pile in back, the building was originally built to be a small machine shop for a company that mined silicone from the river banks to use for auto glass. The man-made caves where the silicone mines had been lay randomly along the river, their openings a series of open-mouthed surprised expressions that are, like the good father's kitchen, hidden to those who forget to look for them. On the coldest days, the days where exposed skin will freeze in seconds, the bums will skip the kitchen and huddle in the caves. It was a bitterly cold day when Father McKenzie, officially a part of the archdiocese of St. Paul and a Franciscan, first realized just how little meat was in the soup he served.

Knowing that the day would be so cold that he would have few, if any, mouths showing up to be fed, Father George McKenzie took his time rousing himself from his warm bed in the small living quarters of the building. He stood, stretched, cracked his lower back, and stared into a mirror. The face of an old man stared back at him, and McKenzie wondered how the boy he had always thought himself to be had ever come to be this old man. He splashed some water on his face and turned the thermostat of the building up a few degrees. On warmer days, he could keep it set at about sixty-six, counting on the heat of the ovens and bodies waiting to be fed to warm the place up to a more comfortable climate. Today would be empty all day. Cold. Quiet. A good day to take inventory, watch TV, and get some of the cleaning done that would involve moving heavy items around.

A few hours later, he looked over his inventory paperwork. As always, every count was perfect. Nothing over, nothing under.

He learned early in his career as a priest that his primary tasks would involve pushing paper, and he learned to do it well. Requisition forms, inventories, and other assorted boring items that needed to be attended to with any organization as large as the Catholic Church all fell to the lower level priests of the archdiocese. It was boring work, and McKenzie often found himself wondering what life would have been like if he had chosen another path. Maybe now he could be living in a huge house, pushing paper for a big company that handed out big paychecks. Ah, but the simple life... it had him in its grips and he knew it would never let go. He smiled to himself, and decided to make some soup for lunch.

Broth. A few noodles. Some tiny chunks of pink stuff the company who sold the soup liked to call meat. McKenzie thought of the bums in the caves, shivering, huddling close to each other and each one wondering if the person next him would be a friend, try to kill him, or just tip over and stop breathing. It was a hard life those men had, and McKenzie tried to mentally keep an inventory of them as they showed up to eat. A winter like this one, with so many days that were so horribly cold... the inventory would dwindle. He looked at the meat again. Protein—real protein, not tiny pink cubes—would help those men. The parish had meager funds, and once McKenzie had been assigned to the kitchen, with its assembly of wretched souls and simple mission to feed them, he had been almost completely forgotten about by every other priest who was busy pushing paper. That was the way he liked it. As long as he kept quiet, stayed hidden under this rail bridge, and never asked for an increase in funds, those who ran the archdiocese left him completely alone.

He sipped his soup, never thinking to question why he chose this life, why he never ate anything different than the bums ate, or why he never bothered to offer them a Sunday mass. The quiet of the kitchen was broken by the tiniest sound. McKenzie cocked his head to one side, not even sure if he had heard it. But then, there it was again. A light *scratch scratch scratch* at the back door. That side of the building's exterior was mostly a jumble of junk items, like old couches, washing machines, and the like. The back door had a large pile of these things crammed up against it, and McKenzie felt sure that no bum could be out there. He went to the front door, opened it, and immediately retreated inside again when he saw no hungry mouth, but felt the harsh cold slap him in the face and pull the air out of his lungs.

He came back to where he had sat in the kitchen, and sure enough, there the sound was again. Scratching at the back door. This time, he was sure of its location. McKenzie didn't even know if the back door was capable of opening, but he turned the deadbolt and then the handle to try. Sure enough, he could push the door open about six inches. As he did so, a train of three kittens ran inside. They were all shivering and began mewing at him as soon as they were through the threshold. He closed the door and looked down at them. He asked, "How did you even know that was a door?"

Rather than answer, the kittens tried to scramble away from McKenzie, but the cold and an obvious case of starvation mixed with worms slowed them greatly. McKenzie couldn't have known it, but the kittens weren't scratching because they wanted in through the door; they were pawing at their mother, dead of the cold and an infection, who lay just outside of where McKenzie could see.

He grabbed the first two pretty easily, but by the time he had done so, the third one had thawed enough to put some speed under the pads of his tiny feet. He took off running, and when McKenzie gave chase, the kitten jumped up onto the table to try and find something to climb for safety. It ended up sprinting directly into the bowl of hot soup, yowling in surprise and shock, then darting away to McKenzie's living quarters. The priest continued his chase, dropping one of the other cats. The chase ended quickly in his bedroom, when the kitten tried to hide inside one of McKenzie's gardening boots.

With two cats in hand and one on the loose again, he went back to the dining area to try and find the last loose kitten. He stopped in his tracks when he saw it sitting at the soup bowl, lapping up the thin brothy mix that McKenzie had been eating for lunch. The M on the little cat's forehead seemed to shine under the florescent lights. The thought struck McKenzie again. *Protein. If the bums had protein, they could stand a better chance against the cold.*

McKenzie closed his eyes tight and shifted the two kittens he held so that he had a small cat head in each fist. Then, as he had learned to do growing up on a small South Dakota farm, he whipped his arms in short, powerful circles to wring their necks. He dropped the two carcasses to the ground, looked to the cat lapping up his soup, and said, "Heeeeere, kitty."

Tender. So tender that the bums without teeth had no problem with it. The cats were small and made mostly of bone and fur, so the little meat there was went into only one batch of soup the next day, but the tiny chunks of pink material the soup company called meat were complemented well by the tender flesh of the kittens. As McKenzie ladled it up for the hungry mouths before him, he began to wonder what in the world the soup company actually *was* putting in there.

After lunch, McKenzie followed his usual routine: Get the bums out so he could clean, get the place ready for dinner, then start cooking the next meal. He looked at the large trash bin that sat in the back of the kitchen, taking note of the bones and fur there. The junk pile out back always had cats in it. No matter what happened, no matter how many of them got killed by disease or cold or a shifting and collapsing pile of debris, there were always more to follow. He pictured the inside of the junk pile as some sort of cat apartment building, where toms roamed the halls and mated with every queen they passed. It seemed to be a basically endless supply of the tender meat that gave the bums warmth and made them smile.

McKenzie trotted to his living quarters, eyes bright. He grabbed his car keys and went out to the lonely compact Japanese car that the archdiocese had given him to use when he needed to run errands. It complained immensely when he turned the key, but in the end, decided to do its job and start. McKenzie drove the squeaky, salt-covered car to the hardware store on 7th and bought three live traps. The kid behind the counter rang them up and asked, "Watcha catchin'?"

McKenzie scowled at him. "Raccoons. Or maybe cats. Something keeps knocking over my garbage cans."

The kid nodded. "Yeah, both will do that. Try putting some fried chicken leftovers in the trap. Cats and raccoons both like those."

McKenzie smiled. "Thanks. I'll do that."

Check the traps in the morning before getting ready for the noon meal. Shoot the cats in the head with a pellet gun—wringing their necks only lasted until the first one bit the priest on the hand. Clean and prepare the catch (McKenzie actually did catch a raccoon once and decided to try to shoot it with the pellet gun; it took another six pellets to finally knock the thing off), and then make the noon meal. It became just another part of the daily routine. As he had suspected, there was no shortage of meat each morning, the traps having been baited with a bowl of cheap cat food each previous night. The bones went into an old grinder that McKenzie had in a storeroom. He had found it back there years ago, and assumed that at some point a previous caretaker of the kitchen had used it to make sausage. McKenzie would throw in the bones, grind them up, and then mix the powder into a bag of fertilizer. He was pretty sure that they would feed his plants well. The furry hides were mixed into the trash.

The meat, he was sure, was helping. Winter chugged slowly along, and McKenzie was noticing that for the first time in months, the sun was up before he was finished with his simple daily breakfast of eggs and toast with coffee. The bums all looked a bit healthier, and his mental inventory of them stayed at a steady count. All was well for the father, all was well for the bums.

And then Mumbles showed up. Father McKenzie called about nine bums Mumbles; it was hard not to make it a common nickname. These were men who were missing most or all of their teeth, had face and mouth injuries, and had been ravaged by disease, drugs, and insanity. This version of Mumbles was a man brown enough to look like he was probably African, but not quite brown enough for McKenzie to be positive. He ended every sentence with something that sounded like "da-ya!" He would yell it out loudly, no matter how calm the mumbly words before it were.

It was the afternoon of a fierce blizzard, one of the last of the season, McKenzie hoped. There was a light tapping at the front door while McKenzie sat in the kitchen, dicing meat for the soup. The tapping was so light, that at first he thought maybe another clowder of kittens wanted shelter, so he went to the back door of the kitchen and opened it the six inches it would give. Nothing.

Then, lightly, another tap. McKenzie knew that it was too early for any of the bums to come around—they may be crazy, but by golly they knew the rules when it came to dinner. He opened the front door, and Mumbles immediately pushed his way in, hugging himself around the shoulders and shivering. Mumbles usually wore a thick yellow stocking cap with a yarn ball on top and a torn-up wool coat. Today he had on a tee shirt and bare head. His thick, tangled nest of black hair looked almost as thick as the stocking cap he usually wore, but it was covered in ice.

Mumbles stood shivering in front of McKenzie, then pointed outside and said, "Num ga dole my doe, da-ya!"

"Okay. Come on in and I'll see if I can find you another one in the donation box. Sit down there." McKenzie pointed to one of the empty dining tables, an old fold-up model from an elementary school that closed down years earlier. The brown plastic veneer was crackled in many places, and there were still faded spots from attempts to bleach out things like "Adam loves Sandy", or "Mr. Ladd is gay."

McKenzie went to the donation storage room that also served as a broom closet off the dining room, and rummaged around. Mittens. Not what Mumbles had come for, but he could use a pair. A couple of baseball caps. No stocking caps, but maybe an old ball cap could do the wretch a bit of good by keeping his head dry. The only coats were kids' sizes, far too small for the man that McKenzie judged to be about six foot two.

He tucked the mittens and cap under this left arm, pulled the door shut, and turned to present them to Mumbles. McKenzie looked to where the man had been sitting, and saw an empty table. He had felt no draft come and go, so he knew the man was still in the building. McKenzie walked to the kitchen, where he had been dicing up meat, and saw Mumbles staring back and forth from the cutting board on the counter to the trash can full of hides. Back and forth, eyes wider each time. Counter to trash, trash to counter. Mumble's jaw dropped a bit more agape each time, his bright red toothless gums shining with spit. His mouth looked like the caves along the river as ice melted around their openings in the spring.

The bum heard McKenzie and turned his head to look at him. He pointed at the hides. "Nu fee uh gas, da-ya!"

McKenzie felt his neck and face flush, and he dropped the mittens and cap. They landed softly on the floor, but to McKenzie the almost imperceptible sound was a loud, crashing *thud!* "Now, Mum- uh, I mean, my son..." He stammered out a few more random syllables, then just clamped his jaw shut and huffed out a sigh. Mumbles just stood there pointing at the hides, his toothless, gaping mouth issuing out an odor of rot that now started to reach McKenzie. The preist started over. "It isn't what it seems like. Really. Come and sit down, and I'll tell you."

Mumbles looked back to the trash, then to the counter, then to McKenzie. He finally closed his mouth, and slowly shook his head. He wanted to be nowhere near the priest who had been feeding him cat meat. McKenzie stood still, the closest he'd ever been to a standoff. He bent down, and picked up the mittens and cap. "I'm still your priest. I still want you to be warm. Take these."

Mumbles backed away a step, looking at the cap and mittens with heightened suspicion, almost as if he thought *those* might be made of cat as well. McKenzie mirrored his movement, taking a small step forward. Mumbles shook his head again, a bit quicker this time. He looked over his shoulder, wondering if the door behind him might lead him to safety.

McKenzie wondered what the man was looking at now. The priest's body acted somehow independently of his mind, and he quickly stepped forward and pinned the man against the kitchen's back door. Mumbles turned and looked McKenzie in the eyes. McKenzie saw a pair of eyes he had never seen this man possess before. They were sharp, the irises narrowed almost to points. Mumbles, in a voice that had passed the edge of panic, shouted out "Bada, doo ba ma, da'ya!"

McKenzie dropped the cap and mittens again, this time hearing nothing when they hit the floor. His body continued on auto pilot, as his hand swiftly reached out, snatched the knife he had been dicing cat meat with, and punched forward. Mumbles recognized the heat of the stab wound—it was his fourth. He looked down to the point where the long chef's knife (donated by a very nice young woman who couldn't get anyone to buy her mother's knife set during the estate sale), protruded out of his body, just below the bottom of his breast bone. Mumbles immediately knew the stab wound was trouble. Two of his other experiences on the sharp end of a knife had been straight punctures like this, but one had gone into his left butt cheek and the other into his right shoulder. Neither had been deep. The other stabbing had been a slashing wound to his chest that didn't do much damage.

Mumbles stared down at the handle of the knife, buried deep into his abdomen. The inside of his body felt incredibly, suddenly, fatally hot as blood gushed into the space that had previously been empty between his various internal organs. He looked back up to McKenzie with wide, wet eyes and sunk slowly to the floor.

McKenzie backed away, unable to take his eyes off of the bum. He could see that the man was trying to mumble out more words, but nothing came. In a few seconds, it was over and the eyes that stared out at him were even more dead than they had been when this man walked in the door.

McKenzie knew what had to happen, and he had to work fast. He pulled out the knife, washed it off in the sink, thought about the best way to fillet the body, and how best to use the meat that he was sure would be tough, grizzled, and quite possibly laced with whatever drugs the bum had taken over the years.

Only three bums for supper. That was three more than he had expected with such a harsh blizzard outside. Mumbles hadn't been cut up yet, so McKenzie had him in the walk-in cooler, waiting for processing. The three tonight got their cat soup, and one asked if he could stay overnight. McKenzie told him that was against the rules, and sent the man on his way. He hoped the man would live through the night to enjoy another meal.

Processing the bum after moving him back out to the kitchen—he had to think of it as "processing" in order to actually bring himself to cut the meat from the man's bones—was the filthiest work Father McKenzie thought he had ever done. It was completely unlike cutting up the cats, because this man was so completely and utterly filthy. He reeked more and more as McKenzie stripped off his clothes, and twice the priest gagged and thought he would vomit. The worst part was when he pulled off the man's underwear. It must have been on him for months. The old boxer shorts were stained horrid colors, and sight of the bum's withered, piss and shit soaked crotch was enough to force McKenzie out of the kitchen to gather himself. In the end, McKenzie decided that more than just bones would have to go in the grinder. With the cats, he could just boil off the remaining flesh from them, but these bones were much larger, and the priest didn't think he could spend the hours it would take to cut away any meat from the face, toes, and other thinly-fleshed areas. He decided to wear gloves to cut away Mumble's genitals; he couldn't stand the thought of touching them skin to skin.

In the end, he had a stack of meat strips that would be enough for five or six day's worth of soup. He had eaten the cat soup; it wasn't half bad. He stared at the pile of Mumblemeat and wondered if he would try to eat it. He decided to see how the bums reacted to it first. He *was* a bit curious about what it would taste like. In seminary, he had always been fascinated with martyrs who had been cannibalized.

He made a quick run to the nearest fleet and farm supply store to pick up ten rolls of butcher paper. Why he bought so much was a mystery even to himself, but he just felt like he wanted to have plenty. The teenage girl with a mouth full of steel braces who stood at the register smiled at him. McKenzie smiled back, noticing the hard nipples that decorated the mounds under her sweater where her large, perky breasts hung. This had no salacious effect on him, and for a second he wondered why in his entire career as a priest he had never regretted the vow of celibacy. "That's a lot of paper," she said in a slobbery *these damn braces are killing me* voice.

"Yeah, uh... My son. He's quartering a cow tomorrow and he needs more."

"My dad always goes through a bunch of that stuff every year when he butchers deer. That'll be thirty-two fifty."

The walk-in cooler, usually almost completely bare, looked nice with the stacks of wrapped white packages of Mumblemeat. The butcher paper was held closed with blue strips of painter's tape. McKenzie was sore, but knew he had to attend to the waste. There was a soupy, sloppy pile of ground material in the sink waiting to be taken care of, and McKenzie wondered if it would all go down the drain. He put on a new pair of latex gloves (the thought of the bum's genitals still disturbed the priest), and ran his fingers through the goop. It seemed thin enough. McKenzie swallowed with a dry throat, steeling himself to be up all night if a backup plan was called for, and turned on the tap.

The thin, demolished flesh and flecks of bone ran down the drain easier than he thought they would. After they were all gone, McKenzie decided to let the water run another ten minutes to make sure everything went down all the way to the sewer. This close to the river, drain backups weren't uncommon.

Days of soup. Strips of Mumblemeat boiled until they were able to be easily eaten by the mass of gummy mouths that lined up to be fed. It was the last meal of Mumblemeat soup, and McKenzie decided that instead of cooking himself a separate small pan of the unadulterated stuff like he had been doing the last few nights, tonight he would try it. The bums seemed to like it.

The closest comparative taste he could think of was pork. Chewy, but not too tough after the long boiling. Tomorrow, it was back to cat. McKenzie watched as the bums began filtering out. He thought again of how odd it was that a hungry mouth, no matter how crazy the mind above it, knows the rules. He sat at the table, staring at his empty bowl long after the dining room was empty. Next would be dishes. Then check the live traps. McKenzie smiled, thinking of a white cat with black spots that had looked so much like a cow that while he butchered it, he pictured himself as a giant, stealing the local villagers' cattle for his meals.

It was almost the end of February, and there were still many rolls of butcher paper in the pantry. McKenzie decided to walk along the river before checking the traps to take in some extra night air. It was warm out, maybe almost forty degrees, even after dark. The bums would be out. He could compare his mental inventory of who came into the kitchen to who was out enjoying the night air. McKenzie didn't really know why he wanted to do this; it wasn't his usual routine.

The park along the Mississippi river in St. Paul is long and narrow, a strip of natural beauty that is bordered on one side by the large river, covered in snow and ice for most of the winter, and on the other side by Lowertown and then downtown. McKenzie watched a small group of bums as they stood near the edge of the river. He approached them, and they said hello, recognizing the priest. It was a pleasant night to be out.

McKenzie headed back before a chill could set in past his thin coat, and as he walked toward his kitchen, he swung wide around to the back of the building. Sure enough, he heard a pair of caterwauls. More than just the tiny cubes of meat for soup tomorrow.

He bent down to open the first trap, when a voice in the dark behind McKenzie startled him. "Watcha doin'?"

McKenzie jumped a bit, stood up straight and turned around to see a rare and elusive creature in his world: a homeless *woman*. She hadn't even been beaten to a pulp any time recently. McKenzie smiled. Most of his bums were men. The few women who came in disappeared soon enough, killed off at a faster pace than the men. This one looked about in her mid thirties. Not ugly, but definitely aged beyond her years and not what anyone would call a fine specimen of the female form. He smiled at her and said, "Oh, I've got lots of raccoons out here. They upset the garbage cans."

She looked over his shoulder. "Them look like cats to me, mister."

"Yeah, sure. Cats. Get a lot of those, too."

99

"Whadya do with 'em?" She walked closer, and McKenzie could smell the stale breath that trailed after her gravel-and-glass voice.

"Oh, gosh." He chuckled. "Just let the cats go, I suppose." He bent down, opened the first trap, and let the cat inside sprint off into the night. Standing up, he smiled at her again, then did the same with the next trap. No meat tomorrow other than tiny pink cubes, after all.

"Say, I'm kinda new around here. Took the bus from Chicago." She smiled, her mouth a toothless rag of flesh.

"Oh," he returned, wondering how long it would be before she left him alone to reset the traps, "Long ride."

She nodded. "Yeah. Used all my money to get here. I need a few bucks. Maybe we could make an arrangement."

"Arrangement?"

She nodded again. "I'll blow you for ten bucks. Sex for twenty."

McKenzie was taken aback. In all his years working with the homeless, this was an entirely new situation for him. He sighed, and thought about ways to counsel the woman, bring her to understand God's role for her. God's role. For her. God's plan. God's plan for her, on a cold night, when there was no meat for the next day. McKenzie smiled, and motioned to the kitchen. "Why don't we go inside? It's warm there."

She looked to the building. "You live here?"

He nodded. "It's my kitchen." They walked around to the front door and went inside, then he led her through the dining room to the back of building, where the kitchen stood clean, quiet, and empty. It was filled with the pure white light of a nightmare. Now and then, one of the overhead fluorescent lights would tick. McKenzie turned to face the woman. In the light, he could see that she wasn't as old as he first thought. She was in her early twenties, but ravaged by meth. She smiled at him, and he could see cankers on her lips. Breath so bad it almost gassed out as yellow mist from behind the smile.

She unbuttoned her pants. "Do you want me naked, or just my pants down?"

"Uh... I want to try something different. Um... turn around." He was nervous. There was absolutely nothing attractive about the creature before him. Judging by the number of sores on her lips, McKenzie thought that anything in her pants would be riddled with bugs, oozing sores, and disease. He watched her as she turned around. Her pants fell to the floor, and he could see that her legs were thin and furry. A few long hairs peaked out from around the boarder of her once red now faded to pink panties.

As quietly as he could, McKenzie reached to the knife block. He slid the large knife he had used on Mumbles out of the block. He knew his senses were on edge again when the sound of the steel blade sliding against the slot of the wood knife block seemed so loud that he thought it would alert people blocks away. The disease-riddled, broken-toothed meal supplement in front of him didn't hear it.

He jabbed quickly to the area that he knew from butchering Mumbles was the right kidney. The *thump* of the knife was followed a grunt of pain. She took a step forward, then slumped to her knees. Bloody urine soaked her panties then ran down her legs as she continued to grunt in pain, on all fours on the floor. Her hands slid out from her sides, and she fell to the floor, breathing faster and faster as her organs shut down. McKenzie stood over her, and looked at her face. Her mouth was curled into a snarl of pain, but her eyes stared unfeelingly up at him. Those eyes didn't beg for mercy, they didn't plead questions of why he had done this. They looked up at him with a resigned expression that said *I knew this was how it would end someday.*

Spring came. The health of the bums seemed to improve more and more, and none of them noticed that one of the group would go missing now and then. One bum lasted weeks when rationed into the soup correctly. By May, the cat population had been ignored for so long by McKenzie that there was a huge clowder in the junk pile. He could hear them yowling at night, reviving the visions of toms stalking through the tunnels in the junk, finding queens and making more and more kittens.

Five bums, then eight. By the time winter came again, McKenzie had processed eleven of them. It was the first night of the winter that was close to zero degrees outside, and he looked at the wrapped packages that were the legacy of number eleven, a young man with brilliant blue eyes. The man had been covered in tattoos, and begged for his life while blood spurted out of a hole in his lower left chest.

McKenzie left the walk-in cooler and went to his room. He turned on the small TV he had from his first assignment as a priest at the Church of St. Lawrence, and lay down on his bunk. "Africa Screams" starring Abbot and Costello was playing. Life here was so simple. A beautiful city, a mission to feed those in need, and everything he needed to do it. He drifted to sleep with a smile on his face, as on the screen Lou Costello stood tied to a pole with natives dancing around him.

The soup the next day was nothing different from any other soup on any other day. The bums should never have known that the supplement to the tiny pink cubes was really strip of Mumblemeat, diced canker girl, or chopped blue eye.

It was a relatively new bum, some guy who always told stories about being an infantryman in Afghanistan, who found it. McKenzie watched as it happened. The man pulled out a long strip of thin meat, and was about to start chewing it when he stopped, stared at it for a second, then turned it ninety degrees. His face vacillated between looks of horror, amazement, reverence, and confusion. Finally, he stood up and pointed to the meat. "Jesus! My soup has the face of Jesus!"

The other bums immediately started gathering around the man. McKenzie started on his way there, and one of the other bums, another Mumbles, looked at him. He pointed down to the strip of meat the man held and said to McKenzie, "Fana! Jeena! Fo' ne-a!"

McKenzie pushed his way through the crowd and looked at the strip of meat. Sure enough, plain as day, the calm, kind face of Jesus stared up at him. The bums all looked to McKenzie for guidance; even though he never wore a uniform and never prayed with them, never gave them a Sunday sermon or had any pictures of Jesus around the building, they all revered him as a priest.

McKenzie recognized the portrait of Jesus from the blue-eyed man's left shoulder. It had been a dark tattoo, and underneath the face of Jesus, it had read "Redeamer". McKenzie had actually laughed out loud at the misspelling, then thought to himself the word should have been "Remeater". On the strip of meat held before him, there were no words. McKenzie looked at the faces surrounding him. "That's nothing, people. Just... a... I don't know. But it isn't a miracle."

The Mumbles who had called him over said, "Ni ih doo!"

McKenzie faced the man. "No, it isn't!"

"Nihe nah?"

"It just isn't, okay? Now give me that!" He reached out for the strip of meat. The bum who had almost eaten it pulled the strip back and held it protectively against his body. Now all of them, somewhere in the neighborhood of thirty to forty bums, stared at McKenzie.

"Look at Jesus," said the bum who held the strip of meat. "Look at his face!" He began showing it to the crowd. They all were nodding, agreeing, and looking back to McKenzie with sharp eyes. They wanted to know why he refused to acknowledge the miracle before him.

It was the one and only woman in the crowd who recognized the tattoo. When she saw the strip of meat, she ran to it, her ratty black-and-gray hair bouncing behind her bruised face and fat lip.

She looked at the meat. "Bobby." She looked back to McKenzie. "This is a tattoo. Bobby had it."

McKenzie slowly shook his head. "You've got to be wrong. Maybe blue eyes had a tattoo, but this could really be a miracle. I, uh, I should take it to the church. You know, have the bishop look at it."

The woman looked sharply at the priest. "What did you call him?"

"Call—" he stopped himself as he retraced his words. He hadn't said Bobby. He had said *blue eyes*. McKenzie backed away, through the circle of bums and back toward the kitchen. "Now just hang on."

The woman looked to the crowd, then mounted the chair in front of her. She pointed to McKenzie. "He's feeding us bad meat! That face of Jesus is a tattoo from my boyfriend! He's been missing since last night."

McKenzie felt his face flush hot and red. "No! No!" He paused, then said the only thing he could think of. "No!"

The man who had discovered the face of Jesus looked at the meat, then back to McKenzie. "How many of us, Father?" They began to advance on the priest, until they encircled him again. Other voices started questioning him, always with the same words. "How many of us father?" Then, so many voices overlapping, it became a cacophony. McKenzie sunk to his knees, lacing his fingers over the back of his head.

A hand grabbed the back of his shirt collar and jerked him to his feet. Slaps, punches, kicks. More hands grabbing his clothes. Lifting him. He kept trying to shout "No!" but every time he tried, his mouth was punched, spit into, and grabbed at by diseased, dirty fingers.

They hauled him to the kitchen and laid him flat on his back on the counter. The questions died down and they quietly stared at him while they held him down. The bum who had found Jesus smashed the piece of meat into McKenzie's face. McKenzie heard the wet meat plop to the floor as the bum turned to face the crowd. "Let's eat him!"

They shouted approvals. McKenzie decided that none of them should feel shame in this; they all had just learned they had been eating people for months now. The knife that had ended eleven of their lives was taken from the block and passed to the woman who once had a boyfriend named Bobby. She looked at McKenzie, then back at the knife. She shook her head and handed the knife to the man who had called for the cannibal action. He looked to the knife, then to McKenzie.

The feeling of the knife across his throat was like accidentally cutting a finger, only a thousand times more painful. Next, the heat inside his esophagus, then the drowning sensation as the hot blood flowed into his lungs and filled them. To McKenzie, it seemed to take so long. To the those in the kitchen, it went so fast.

Sound faded, then light and touch as the priest's brain slowly starved of oxygen.

They were unskilled hands. The grinder was found by the next morning, and they had the mess cleaned up by noon the next day. Hungry mouths know the rules.

Every large can of soup was opened, and they gorged. The crowd lost any sense of propriety for their fallen brother, and Bobbymeat as well as McKenziemeat was thrown into the broth. The father had fed them for years, now he fed them for a day.

The kitchen stood empty, its lights still on. The kitchen and pantry had been raided to emptiness, and a mess of packages, pots, pans, and utensils lay everywhere. It was almost a week before anyone reported the priest missing. Another three weeks before the church decided to just close the kitchen rather than assign another priest there. Two senior paper-pushing priests stood outside of the kitchen, signing documents that would turn the building and land over to the city for any future development.

The first priest, a young man with eyes the color of a dull nickel, turned and looked to the other priest, a man in his late forties. They were both in uniform. "Well, Tom, what do you think happened to him?"

The older priest shrugged. "He might have run off. He was always a little odd. Did you know that he got this assignment because no church would take him?"

"Really? Problems with kids?"

"No, no. Nothing like that. Just kind of a weird guy." A bum shuffled up to them, and tapped the older of the two on the shoulder. The priest turned to the homeless man, and said, "Do you know where Father McKenzie went?"

The homeless man smiled and patted his stomach. He looked to them both and said, "He made good soup." He started laughing, and shuffled away.

Zulu Operator

I stared into the mirror of the small bathroom, listening to the sounds of people ordering subs outside. My hands shook just the smallest bit, and I splashed cool water on my face, ran cold wet hands through my hair. It was always like this after a job.

A few minutes later I was walking out the back door of the sandwich shop, changed out of the jeans and thick black cotton tee shirt and into a pair of light colored linen pants and an equally light button up Hawaiian shirt. I got to the car, a rental Chevy Malibu, and tossed my bag in the back seat. The trunk contained my tool of choice for this job, a .22 caliber rifle in a nondescript black bag. No ammo. I made sure it had all been spent.

On a job like this one I would usually only carry three subsonic rounds. They make a pop about as loud as a popcorn kernel. The small slug is enough, and it usually only takes one shot. Today took two, but that was because I had the windage wrong and slug number one hit the old gal's glasses before deflecting into her forehead. It took her down and she bled a lot, but she kept slowly moving her arms and legs, trying to get up and go. Slug number two did the trick, right through the parietal region of her skull.

In no time I'm on the road. A short drive to the hotel, put the original plates back on the car, a quick drive to a predetermined alley with a dumpster in it, put the stolen plates in the trash, then maybe beer and a dinner. Easy job.

The people I work for are pretty decent. They give me a paycheck every two weeks to train. Go to shooting ranges, research rifles, spend time learning more biology. I've got a PhD now. If I walked up to you on the street and told you that I worked for a government agency called the Reeder Center and that I had my PhD in biology, with a masters in chemistry and three bachelors, you'd probably think I was some kind of intellectual spy. Not me. I'm what's called a "Zulu Operator." For every one of me, there's about three hundred of the geek spies. I get a job every few months, and most of them are out of the country. Pretty odd, in fact, to get one on good old Uncle Sam's front yard.

I get the plates tossed in the trash, and as the sun is setting over Portland, Oregon, I decide to have a little fun. There's this great bar downtown with a cool view of the Columbia. Before that, though, I decide to swing through the rose gardens, catch a good view of downtown while there's still a bit of light. The roses are spectacular today, and I actually break the garden's rules—a big no-no for a guy who lives under the radar—and pick the most beautiful Belle Nanon I've ever seen. The pink bourbon flower looks nice on the gray dash of the Malibu.

An hour later I'm at my favorite bar downtown, enjoying a Buffalo chicken wrap and a cold Workhorse. Portland is one of my favorite cities, and I know it will be about three years before I can even *think* about dropping by again. Best to enjoy a local brew now, while I can. That night in the hotel I lie in bed, turn off the TV and meditate, reliving the job.

***

She walks out onto the back deck at a bit after twelve with a sandwich and a glass of milk, just like she does nearly every day. A target's routines are my best friend. I watch her through my scope, white hair blowing around a face that is still surprisingly pretty for a woman knocking on the door of eighty. The glass of milk makes me clench my teeth a bit, knowing how much easier it would have been to just poison her. Heart attack. She's old. It happens.

But instructions are instructions, and my instruction packet was explicit: Let the world know she was murdered. I know it is part of a larger puzzle, my little piece. Maybe they want to place blame on the mob. Maybe she's in a secret society (there are more of those than you would think) that needs a message sent. Who knows, and who cares? Her file didn't give me any clues about why it had to be murder.

She sits there on her deck, chewing a bite of her sandwich. I squeeze the trigger so gradually that it surprises me when it goes off. Just a small *pop* and her head whips back. I can see by the way her glasses break that I've hit them. Sometimes, that isn't bad. But she's got the high-end stuff, the glasses made strong enough to wear when you ride a cycle or work on a construction job. She's face down, trying to get her hands and feet under her. There's a growing pool of blood, and I've got a good angle on the back of her head. One more *pop* and she's down again. The blood geysers out of her skull about six inches high for two pumps. Then the only blood is coming from the front, somewhere that I can't see. My best guess is that the slug went into her skull and bounced around enough that blood is coming out of her nose and mouth. I can see a bit more trickle from her ear. She's a goner.

Lights out at eleven. A short day tomorrow. I meet my local contact, a young guy named Harry, in a hangar just outside of town. He'll return the car for me. Harry's got long, curly black hair and a goat beard. We shake hands, exchange the usual pleasantries. He's seen the news story about my job, and gives me a pat on the back for a mission completed successfully.

I'm home before you know it. I walk into the large farmhouse I share with my wife, Kelly, and big black mutt of a dog named Max. We never had kids. She smiles when I walk in the door. "How'd it go, Sweety? I missed you."

We kiss after I hand her the rose I picked. "Job went well."

She pours me a glass of lemonade from a pitcher in the fridge. "How many shots?"

"Two. I put the third in a squirrel." Kelly has known about my job for almost all of the twenty-five years we've known each other. The stuff they show you in the movies is ridiculous. I don't have a cover job as a computer repairman or anything like that. I live outside of Indianapolis. My office building, which I only have to go to about three times a month, is hidden in plain sight in a suburb called Avon. It says "Reeder Center" right on the door. There's a dentist in the building next to us. I flirt with the hygienist there when I bump into her on the way to or from lunch.

Kelly makes dinner and I sit outside afterward enjoying another lemonade and contemplating whether or not to play a game of fetch with Max. He looks at me with his mutt eyes, begging. I can hear Kelly inside doing the dishes. I weigh which I want to do more (or less): dry plates, or throw a slobbery tennis ball. The tennis ball wins.

We're well into our game of fetch when a familiar deep blue Buick roles up my gravel driveway. It's my Prime, Jack Knowles. He's been my Prime, or handler as other agencies would say, for over twenty years. Nice guy.

I toss the ball and watch strings of spittle whirl off of it as it flies through the air. Jack is out of the car and walking my way with a smile. Management must be very happy with the mission's results. He waves, and I wave back. For about seventy, the guy looks great. His full head of hair—the only truly beautiful Afro I've ever seen in my life—has only recently turned gray, and his teeth are so white and healthy that they shine in contrast to his chocolate skin. "Good job on the mission, Greg."

I smile back at him as Max drops the ball at my feet. "Thanks, Jack." We shake hands. Max sits near us and woofs out a bark as quiet as he can. He loves Jack. Jack kneels down and pets Max for a bit, then tosses the ball.

I motion my head to the back deck. "Kelly made fresh lemonade. Debrief over a glass?"

Jack nods. "Sounds good. Then I've got something new for you."

We're already walking to the deck. "New? Jeez, Jack, I just got back to town five hours ago. Did we get more intel on that wing of Al-Qaeda in Columbia?"

He shakes his head. "Not that kind of thing, Greg. This is a different mission all together. But first," we sit down and Kelly, who has seen us coming, is already pouring out two glasses, "We debrief. Hi Kelly."

"Hi, Jack." She bends down so that he can kiss her cheek. Turning to me, she asks, "Will you grab me from the den when you're done?"

"Sure thing." She's a good woman. She knows that debrief time often involves classified information, and besides that, when all is said and done, it just isn't cool for a spouse to hang out during this type of business.

***

The sun is down and the automatic light has turned on by the time we're through with the debrief. We look at each other

110

quietly for a minute, and I can tell something is up with Jack. I smile and put up my hands in a gesture that says *I know nothing*, then ask, "Okay, Jack. You're way too quiet. What is it?"

He looks at me very seriously and bites his bottom lip. "Greg, you're fifty-three. Central Management wants to assign you to a training gig."

My jaw drops. "Jesus Christ, Jack, I can't retire! I'm the best you've got!"

He nodded. "That's true, Greg. And that's, I think, why Central wants to move you to training. How many assignments did you have in your first twenty years?"

I lean back and think for a few seconds, doing quick math in my head. "I suppose about two dozen."

"And in the last ten?"

I shrug. "Okay, about the same number."

He puts his finger on the side of his nose and then points it at me. "We're using you twice as much. That's high demand for your type of talent, Greg."

"How many new guys are you bringing in? And where from?"

"Well, it's new *people*; not all of them are guys. We're getting them primarily from special forces, but we worked with NSA to set up a special database for young people who take the foreign service exam and also fit the profile for a Zulu Operator." Before I can ask any more questions, Jack reaches into his pants pocket and pulls out his car keys. "I've got your mission packet in the trunk. You can accept and start training on Monday, or you can decline. If you decline, I have another packet for you. Instead of instructions about where to go and how to begin your new assignment, it has all kinds of thrilling information about your pension, and finding civilian work that is acceptable to Central Management."

"Let me guess. None of the acceptable civilian jobs have anything to do with security, consulting, or law enforcement."

He nods. "That's right."

"And breaking those protocols," I continue, "Means loss of pension.

111

He nods again. "Four thousand a month, tax free, down the drain."

I huff out a frustrated sigh, and lower my forehead to my palms. "I suppose it isn't that bad. Do I at least get a raise?"

"It's a good bump. Twenty percent. That puts you at about two hundred a year."

I shrug. "I wish I had kids to leave some of it to."

Jack smiles. "Greg, you know you're the oldest Zulu we've got. You should have been assigned to training five years ago, maybe even longer back then that. With the emphasis on black ops, the higher budgets we're getting, and the plethora of targets out there..." he shrugs his shoulders.

"You need new guys."

"We need people like you to train the new... *people*."

I sigh again. "Okay. I'll take the training gig. Just please don't assign me a woman."

Jack smiles and chuckles. "Okay, buddy. I'll make sure your first Tango is a man."

***

That night is sleepless. At four I get out of bed, and Max follows me to the study. I sit down and start making notes about things I will need to train the Tango—trainee. *Let's see... he'll need to know what subjects to start learning on his own. I probably shouldn't tell him what to study until I get to know him a bit. Oh, that's another note to self. I'll need to spend the first few days building a profile of the Tango; by the end of a month, I'll want to know more about what makes him tick than he knows about himself.* I make notes like this for almost an hour, then return to bed.

As I'm climbing in and Max is settling back onto the rug beside Kelly, she props herself up on an elbow and gives me a sleepy smile. "It'll be fine, Greg. Just a little different."

"I haven't kept you up all night, have I?"

She smiles. "No worries. I'll call in sick. We'll spend a long weekend together." With that, she leans in and kisses me. I realize for about the millionth time how wonderful she is, and before I know what's happening, we're making love. Afterward I sleep

112

more soundly than I have in days, and I don't wake up until almost nine.

The weekend is terrific. We do some shopping, hit a few antique shops. At night, we share drinks, and talk about life. I wonder sometimes if having kids would have made times like this impossible. Max is my shadow, his tail's constant sway a reminder of how happy he is that I am home. He and Kelly both tell me with their behavior that the end of my traveling days will be a sweet relief.

Monday morning. I wear my usual office garb, a polo and comfortable dress slacks. Mary, the receptionist, smiles and wishes me luck. The email announcing my "promotion" has already been sent out. My desk is completely empty when I get to it, and I wonder for a second who the hell the prankster is before I remember from my packet that I now have an office on the second floor.

I spend the morning making my new office homey. I'm down the hall from Jack, who is being assigned a new Tango today, too. He drops in as I'm taking various military field manuals out of boxes and arranging them on a shelf. "Hey, Greg. So how do you like the new digs?"

"Good. They're good." I look around. I've got a window now that looks out over a small park in back where people who work in the area often have lunch. "I've got a view." Jack steps in and sits in the comfortable leather chair that I now possess for visitors. Sighing, I tell him "I have no idea what to do now, Jack."

He laughs. "Neither did I when you were assigned to me. I don't today, either. It always goes that way when you get a new Tango. Even though I'll be training someone new myself, you can still count on me to walk you through the training process. You'll do fine." Jack smiles at me, and I feel so much more at ease. He knows what he's doing, and he's going to be right down the hall. "Want to come down to Central Management with me? They've got the files for our new Tangos."

"Sounds good."

An hour later, I'm behind my desk reading a four-inch thick file on a young Navy SEAL named Mark Bertrand. I prep for this assignment the same way I prep for—*used to* prep for, that is—a job. I'll learn everything I can about him, what makes him tick. I've got to figure out what to tell him to study, what areas he thinks are strengths that are really weaknesses, and how important it is to live a normal life.

It's Thursday before I've got my own training plan completed for him. One full year, then a reevaluation. He's in my office on Friday, knocking on the open door before he passes through the threshold. He's lost a bit of weight since the last photo of him in the file. Five-eleven, two hundred and ten pounds. Dark hair cropped too close to his scalp to mean anything but military duty. Green eyes. He's wearing a green dress shirt and black wool slacks. I wave him in and say, "Close the door, Mark."

I stand. We shake hands. He's got a good, strong grip and a big smile. I motion to the leather chair. "Take a seat."

He sits, and leans forward a bit. I can tell he's excited. "It's really nice to meet you, Sir."

I twirl a pen through my fingers. "Mark, two rules to start out. First, don't call me Sir. You're done with the military. I need you to blend. By the time training is done, you won't raise any eyebrows walking through a poppy market in Islamabad. Rule number two: Grow out your hair. If you can grow a beard, even better."

Mark runs his hand over his nearly bald scalp. "I just got a high and tight before I left base."

"You're a civilian now. When you go to Belize, you need to look like some surf bum who has too much of his daddy's money and wants to scuba dive. When you go to Hong Kong, you need to look like a businessman who only works out because it keeps his wife from riding the mailman while you're out of town. Got it?"

"Yes, Si—uh, yeah. Got it. What do I call you? Mr. Martinsen?"

"Greg. Call me Greg. I've known my mentor for over twenty years, and we're practically best friends. You and I will need to get that close. Right now, you're a Tango Operator. A trainee. Once you're a Zulu Operator, I not only continue training you, but I become your backup support."

"Okay. So what do I need to know about you to start?"

"First, that Central Management matched us together because we have similar personalities. Or at least, they think we do. I've read your file, and I agree that we're probably a good match. We're both married. You've got a two-year-old, but I don't have any kids." When I mention the baby, he shifts in his seat a bit. I stare at him, wanting him to tell me what is on his mind, but not willing to just come out and ask.

He says, "Can I ask you a personal question, Greg?" I nod. "Did you skip kids because of the job?"

I smile, realizing that I need to put him at ease. Even though he's been in the Special Forces for almost ten years, this is a completely different world. He probably still is holding on to the Hollywood image of the job: Skulking around at night, avoiding being assassinated yourself by rouge agents, other bullshit like that. "Kelly and I always wanted kids. We just aren't able. That's her in that picture there."

"She's pretty."

"Thanks. We met when I was just about to finish my time with Delta Force. She was a waitress and undergrad student. She's a chemist now. Your wife, Kara, she's an accountant, right?"

He nods. "Yeah. Looking for some work in town here that she can do from home."

We stare at each other for a few seconds. I shift back into work mode, and say, "Okay, so a few basics about the job. You will spend most of your time in the office, on the range, or in a classroom. We've got a few training locations around town for you to work on your hand-to-hand combat skills, as well."

He smiles and nods. "I'm pretty good with a knife."

"Then take up making sushi. Most of your jobs are going to be done in a manner that makes the world think your target died due to accident, disease, or something in the middle. I've got over forty kills. Want to know how many of them anyone in the real world thinks were assassinations?"

115

"Well, given what you just told me… I'd guess about ten percent."

"Smart man, Mark. Five kills were something that looked like something other than fate. The last one was an old lady who ran a bus company in Oregon."

He nods again. "They showed me the file during orientation. The Portland police are blaming some Russian mobsters who came to town recently."

"I didn't know that."

"Really?"

"Really. I put some space between myself and the job afterward. I don't spend time trying to figure out why I got the assignment. So your first three weeks are all office time, then we'll start to hit ranges and pick out course work. Your undergrad in Psychology will be a nice help with profiling your assignments. How did you do at chemistry?"

"Only got a C." He shrugs and looks embarrassed.

"Not a problem. Biology?"

"I took a few courses, mostly stuff like sensation and perception. A's and B's in each class."

"Good. We'll start there. Plan on two night classes a week for the rest of your career, until you move from a Zulu Operator to a Prime. You get a ton of vacation with this job. It helps make up for spending fifty hours a week with your nose in books." I notice that he's shifting around in his seat again. "What's up, Mark?"

He blushes slightly. "Well, this being my first day and all… I don't know where the bathroom is."

I can't help but laugh. I like the guy. "They haven't set up your cube yet or told you which parking spot is yours, either, huh?"

He shakes his head. "They said that today and tomorrow would be kind of office orientation days."

"Okay. I'll show you around."

"Bathroom first?"

"Yeah, bathroom first. Plan on bringing your wife in tomorrow."

In a surprised voice, he asks, "She can see the place?"

"It's an office, Mark. She can see the place, and she needs to know what you do for a living. Don't keep secrets from her unless we order you to."

***

His first two months are almost all cerebral. He's learning Swahili and brushing up on his Spanish. He doesn't need to be fluent, but he's got to know enough to get around effectively. We've got him enrolled in a Master of Science program studying biology. His hair is coming along well, but he hates the idea of a beard. I understand, never having been able to get used to one, myself.

We meet at the heavy weapons range at sunrise. Over a cup of coffee, we start a discussion about the three heavy rifles he can use for a long-range job. I point to the first rifle. "Recognize this?"

"Thirty caliber. Belgian made." He pauses, looking closely at the scope. "I've never seen this scope before. Why is it square?"

The scope is indeed square. It looks like a thick, long, black plastic box. "Look through it." He picks up the rifle and peers through the scope. This is the first time I've seen him hold a firearm. He's a natural at it, and the rifle looks like it has grown out of his very body. "Now move the selector lever two clicks." He pulls his cheek away from the butt to look at the selector lever on the rifle. It is marked *SAFE* then *FIRE 1*, then *FIRE 2*. He welds his cheek to the butt again, and shifts the selector to *FIRE 2*.

"Whoa!" He looks all over the room through the scope, then out a window with it. The firing range outside is empty, reserved for us for the next six hours. "It that the building wiring?"

"Right. What else do you see in the walls?"

"Looks like hot and cold spots. This thing is obviously thermal... but focused on wiring. There goes a mouse."

"It's focused on wiring, you're right. Why?"

He sets the rifle down after shifting the selector lever back to *SAFE* and thinks for a few moments. "I suppose if I need to take out the electricity. But why not just tune the thermal to really pop when it sees a body?"

"Keep thinking. Remember what we've been talking about. Your primary weapon. What is it?"

"Brain."

"Right. So this thirty cal is secondary. You can knock out the power a thousand different ways."

"Yeah..." He's thinking more, really turning it over in his head. "But with this, I can knock out the power from four, maybe five hundred yards." He sits down, and runs his fingers over the rifle. "Say I'm five hundred yards out. That means I don't want to get close. Or can't get close. After everything is said and done, anyone investigating will find the bullet hole and know that it was a round from a rifle that... I've got it." He looks to me, smiling his big smile. "Security systems. Where I've got to bring the system down and just get the hell out of Dodge. Maybe shut off a system that keeps explosives safe, or turn off computer systems for the tech goons to do some hacking."

I nod toward the rifle. "I used that model of rifle and scope to shut down the cooling system on a drug lord's liquid oxygen system. Everything blew to hell. The drug lord's scientists, all eight of them, were incinerated."

"Wow."

"That's why a certain Columbian drug lord doesn't send spy satellites into orbit, even though he's got the money to do it. We missed out on his sub program by about six weeks. He's been using the damn things to ferry drugs up from the east coast of South America."

Mark gives me another one of his big smiles. "I took one out." I raise my eyebrows at him, and he reads the question on my face. "We tracked one of their routes and patrolled it in an old fishing boat we rigged with a couple of short-range torpedoes and a fifty cal. I pegged it with the fifty for about ten rounds. Glub, glub."

"Nice!" A high five. "Speaking of fifties, what do you think of rifle number two?"

Mark looks down to the black metal on the table in front of him. He smiles, and runs his finger tips along the barrel the way he probably would run them up and down his wife's legs. A rush of air flows out of his nostrils, and they flare slightly. Before he speaks, I know that he's loved this weapon since before he knew it existed. Of all his weapons, heavy, light, hand, mechanized, or anything else, this will be his favorite. He looks up to me, eyes more focused than I've seen yet. "Special order. No manufacturer markings, but it resembles the fifty cal rifles I've seen in the field that are manufactured by Colt." He picks it up, feels its weight and looks through the scope. "Red dot scope, accurate for at least a mile, probably more like a mile and a quarter. Effective kill range the same." He runs the bolt twice, and I know that the snap of the mechanism makes his heart pound harder. "The bolt gives it more reliability and accuracy. This is a one-shot-one-kill weapon. It isn't made for electrical installations, it isn't made for stealth. This is pure power, accuracy, and distance."

"Give me three situations where it is ideal." I throw out pop quizzes like this constantly. He handles all of them the right way: He thinks when he needs to, and is always coachable if he gets one wrong. He nails this one.

"One: Your drug lord. Find his compound, camp outside of it in the jungle until you get your shot. The distance, vegetation, and surprise allow you enough time to get out. Two: Hostage taker. With this scope and the accuracy of an EXACTO round, you can take him out even if he is almost completely shielded by a hostage. Three: Anti-vehicle. A fifty caliber slug weight of 52 grain will crack most engine blocks and can take down an aircraft."

"You like this weapon?"

He sets it down on the table and caresses it again. "I feel like it was made for me."

I smile. "It was. These three are yours. Now, if you can take your eyes off of your new lover there, see what you can tell me about heavy weapon number three."

Mark looks at the twenty-two and furls his brow. "Do we assassinate many ground hogs?"

I laugh, genuinely tickled at this. "This is what I used for my last job. You gave me three scenarios where the fifty is king, now give me three for this little gal."

"This is seriously considered a heavy weapon?" I nod. He continues, saying, "Okay. Well, let me think. You told me you used

119

this on that Portland job. I think that was a hint. This would be quiet."

"Really quiet if you pack the round light enough," I hint to him.

"Bingo! No bang. When you need to get in close and can't haul ass out of there."

"Okay, there's number one. Two more times this is the right weapon."

"Number two…" I can see that he's struggling, but I let him work it out. "Number two. An 'accidental' shooting, like a hunting accident. Most of my kills will have to look like the person was never meant to die."

"Good. Number three."

"Number three." He rubs his chin. "You've got to get a pretty clean hit with this thing to kill. Put it in the skull, and it'll bounce around and tear the brain to hell. Put it anywhere else, and it'll probably have a high survivability rate."

"You're on the right track, Mark."

"I suppose if you just wanted to wound someone, while keeping the option of putting some lead in their brain pan if things got hairy…"

"Exactly! A snatch and grab is still a snatch and grab if your target has some lead in his leg, as long as he's breathing."

***

Another six months go by. His languages are coming along excellently. On the range, he can hit a four square-inch target at just under a mile with the fifty cal. It's time for some field practice.

I offload from the private jet on a large proving ground in northern Minnesota. It's the middle of summer, and there are tons of guardsmen and reservists in the field for their two week annual training. I get a lot of looks as I walk off the plane. These men and women are teachers, mechanics, students. I have a cover story that I am from a company that supplies helmets, and I need to spend some time in the field seeing how they perform. I think it's kind of a lame cover, but they wouldn't let me uniform up and pretend to be from the Inspector General's office.

Mark drove to the area in a rented SUV. His mission is simple: Sneak onto the lightly defended base, find a staff sergeant I picked randomly from a file I found in a database, and light the sergeant up. In the language Mark and I use, lighting up the sergeant means hitting him with a laser shot. When the guardsmen are performing their field exercises, they use what is basically a glorified laser tag system. The M16s are outfitted with a laser, and the soldiers wear sensors on their bodies and helmets. When the sensor registers a hit, there's a high-pitched beep and flashing lights to indicate "You're dead, buddy."

Mark has had six weeks to prepare. I give him the file on Staff Sergeant William Sandkirk, then leave him to his work. I spend the time preparing my own cover, studying training techniques that successful Primes at Reeder have used in the past, and enjoying a simpler life with Kelly. I have wine at night after a home-cooked meal. No more sixteen hour days of studying, target shooting, harsh physical training, and reading files.

I make it to the field exercise where Sandkirk waits. I've set up time with his platoon. I want a mix of soldiers around when his lights and beeper activate. Mark will pass this test if Sandkirk and *only* Sandkirk is hit. He's got his choice of heavy weapon, but is limited to three shots. As I get out of the humvee and approach the group of soldiers who stare at me, irritated that they have to spend time in some sort of helmet focus group, I picture Mark in a tree or the underbrush somewhere, watching me through his scope.

I recognize Sandkirk from his file, but pretend not to know him or have much of an idea of what the stripes and rocker on his shoulder mean. He's a pudgy guy, early thirties. Two tours in Afghanistan. Purple Heart. Three commendations. He smiles at me, his light blue eyes reflecting the genuine pleasure he has in meeting someone new. This is the kind of guy I'd like to have a beer with.

He sticks out his hand and is about to introduce himself when his laser system activates. A little over a second later, there is a faint rumble of thunder that no one but me notices as the sound of the blank reaches us. I recognize the sound as the fifty cal. Mark has to be nearly a mile away judging by the delay between the hit

and the sound. Sandkirk grimaces, and says, "Hold on a second."
He turns around to the men behind him. "Alright, who's the fuckin'
wise guy?" I can't help but smile.

When I meet up with Mark back at Reeder, he's got the
worst case of poison ivy I've ever seen. The doctors on the first
floor are giving him prednisone shots, and plan on vaccinating him
when this round of poison ivy hell has passed. The advantage of
the top secret vaccination is that is also vaccinates the person
against the blister agent the military keeps tucked away in case of
"emergencies." He sees me and smiles. "Did the sergeant even
know what hit him?"

I shake my head and laugh. "He chewed his guys out pretty
good, though. Nice shot, Mark."

***

It's late, almost eleven PM. We study a satellite photo of a
compound in a jungle. I point to a small wooden building behind
the much larger one made of concrete blocks. "This looks like a
well pump room. We could take out the water supply."

Without looking up from the photo, Mark adds, "Or poison
it."

I nod. "Acceptable collateral on this one is anyone and
everyone living in the compound. You'd have to get in close for
that."

"Yeah, but if the intel is right, he's got a few of his top
lieutenants in there with him. Getting in close might be worth the
risk."

"Okay. If you can get inside, poison the well. We should
make it look like a natural event if we can."

"That way whoever takes over for Unti won't think to
guard his wells again. He'll just cap this one and call it bad luck."

"Right. Second option, take out the well and wait outside
to pick off Unti when he decides to move to another safe house."

"Got it. Is there a third option?"

I consider a few possibilities, then say "I'll work with the
boys at the predator base. If Unti doesn't leave, we'll have to use a
drone."

Unti is an African warlord who's been a thorn in the ass of the free world for years. We've finally got his location nailed down. It's a relatively small compound, but it has all the comforts a warlord would want: satellite dish, mobile cell tower, four car garage, and a guest house for sex slaves captured during his last raid. It might sound cruel that the sex slaves are expendable, but chances are they are infected with HIV, and Unti makes a habit of murdering them during sex when he gets tired of them. The Administration has gotten tired of waiting for Unti to get infected with HIV.

The next morning I meet Mark in a small hangar. He's got all of his gear packed, and is ready to board the Reeder private jet that I used to reserve so often. It's a sleek Citation II. I love that plane. Its white wings reach out to me as if to offer a hug from a long-lost friend, and as I pass by it, I run my fingertips along the wingtip fuel pod.

The last of Mark's gear is getting thrown on the plane, and he smiles at me. He dressed smart, wearing jeans and a tee shirt. He's got hiking boots on. He won't put on his jungle gear until he's in the African jungle. I smile at him and hand him a cup of coffee from the local joint between Reeder and the airfield. "First mission."

He nods. "First mission."

"Nervous?"

That brings out a laugh. "Hell no! I've been waiting for this."

The pilot leans out of the door of the jet. She's in her early forties, a retired Air Force pilot. "You ready to go, Mark?"

"Yeah." He turns back to me. "Any parting words of wisdom?"

"Enjoy summer camp, Junior."

"Thanks, Mom." We laugh again, shake hands, and before I know it he's on the plane. In the sky, its wings look silver as the engines pull it away.

***

Codes and code words are simple. Five nights later I get a text at about two in the morning. I sit up in bed and unlock my phone. Two simple words: *Black metal.*

I smile, knowing that Unti is dead. Black metal means he was shot. Mark must have either not been able to get to the well to poison it or caught Unti as he left after someone else got sick from the water. I type the reply: *Calm water.* It means *Good job, come home.*

I'm back asleep in ten minutes; I won't have a chance to talk to Mark until he gets back in about thirty-six hours or so. Before dawn, my phone's text alert wakes me again. It takes me a second to decipher what I see in front of me. It's a text from Jack, and it reads *THUNDERCLOUD.*

Mark is missing.

***

I'm in Jack's office a little under an hour later. Like me, he looks tired and worried. A map of Lagos, Nigeria is electronically displayed on an otherwise white tabletop. Jack and I lean over it. Mark's last known location is marked with a pulsing red dot. Jack points to a pulsing blue dot. "This is where Gardner was kidnapped." Gardner is Mark's local contact.

"How soon after Mark checked in last did we lose Gardner?"

"Ten, maybe fifteen minutes."

"We're sure he was kidnapped?"

Jack nods. "The secretary of the warehouse that we've got him housed in witnessed it. Typical Unti kidnapping operation. A delivery scooter arrived, and asked for Gardner. He came out to get the delivery, and got whacked with a dart. I think they're holding him for information on how we got to Unti."

"So you think they know there's a team."

"Right." Jack looks at me and shakes his head. "Gardner was good cover. I have no idea what happened, Greg."

"I'll find out when I get there."

"Whoa, hold on. This isn't the good old days, buddy. Let's take this thing slowly. Figure out where Gardner slipped up. After we know you can get out there safe, you can track down Mark. Any ideas of where he might be holed up?"

I shake my head. "I haven't gotten any communication from him after mission success. It's only been six hours, so he can't be far from the compound yet."

"You trained him well. Let's take the next six hours to try and find out how Gardner got burned."

Protocol is to wait at least twelve hours after a blown cover to make any communication to Reeder. The fact that I haven't heard anything from Mark means, most likely, that he knows the cover is blown. Alternatively, it could mean that he's dead. The least likely scenario is that he was captured. I count that as least likely, because if Unti's surviving forces had both Gardner and Mark, the CIA would have gotten an emailed ransom demand or beheading video by now.

I head to my office, and open all the files I have on Gardner. He's been running a warehouse in Lagos for almost five years. Chicken supplies. No romantic relationships, no previous cover problems. Then, I see it. Three trips to doctors in Lagos for crabs. He may not have any romantic relationships, but he's having sex. If he's catching something from it, maybe he's paying rather than taking the time and effort to date.

I'm in Jack's office with my theory when the twelve hour mark hits. "Jack, here's what I think happened. Gardner found a prostitute that he liked, and he went back to her multiple times. Eventually, she got some information about him and sold it."

Jack nods, thinking about it. "How did you come up with this?"

"He's had crabs three times in the last four years."

"Okay. Let's hope she didn't know much beyond the fact that he was some sort of operative. I'll call the CIA and see if they've gotten a ransom demand that they haven't told us about yet. If they haven't, that means that whoever is in charge now that Unti is dead is going to be working Gardner pretty hard for information on who pulled the trigger. Looks like you're heading to Lagos. Get in, find Mark. If you can get Gardner out too, do it. If not, leave him."

"I can handle that."

He nods. "Okay, Greg. Book the flights. Be careful."

I turn to leave when my text alert sounds.

***

Beekeeper.

It means he's safe. Hiding out. I reply *Icicle.* It means *stay put, I'm coming.* Jack and I turn back to the electronic map and review the "safe zones" that Mark and I picked before he left. I am going to start my search at the Hotel France.

The flights are long, even on private jets. On the way, Jack calls me and tells me that no agency has received a ransom demand for Gardner. "Okay, Jack. They know that somebody from American intelligence will be coming, so they're going to be watching me from the moment I get off the plane."

"You can count on it. Stick to your cover."

My cover. I hate my cover on this one. I'm a producer for a public radio show, scouting for humanitarian stories. It gives me legitimate access to the places I need to go to find Mark. I remember the conversation we had about blown covers in the weeks leading up to the mission.

Mark had been frustrated. "If another team member gets picked, why can't I just get to the airport, hop on a plane and go?"

"In all likelihood, they'll know when you arrived and what you look like. Remember, you're on their turf, so they've got the intel advantage. You're going to need to get to the airport in the trunk of a car or inside of a crate. If it looks really bad, I'll come and get you."

"I don't need a chaperone, Greg. I was a SEAL, for crying out loud!"

"And now you're a Zulu Operator. If you can make it to the airport, do it. If not, I'll come to you. We'll work together and get you out."

***

When I get off the plane, I know that Unti's men are looking for operatives, and as an American coming in on a private jet, I stick out like a sore thumb. That's actually part of my cover. Most people like Unti or whoever is in charge of his group now

126

expect operatives to fly in with a military group, or under deep layers of cover. With any luck, they see me, do a little research, and decide I'm nothing to worry about. No matter what, they are going to hack my phone so I've been issued a clean one from Reeder. It has none of the previous texts from Mark or Jack in its memory, and has been populated with a ton of bogus texts, pictures, and other information. I send a text to Mark's phone: *Hey, Mark! I finally made it to Lagos. Meet for a drink tonight?*

As an operative, sometimes the best thing that can happen is to get a completely fake invitation for a beer. It means that your Prime has arrived, and wants to meet to get you the hell out of there. The return text comes just a minute later. *Sounds great, buddy. I'll give you a call at seven.*

Good job. No location given, just a time to get more information. A driver waits for me, smiles as I arrive at the curb, and loads my luggage into a black Suburban. We're off to the Hotel France, a luxury hotel downtown.

The air in Lagos is thick with pollution. The entire city stinks of it. I button up my room, crank the air conditioning to get filtered air into the living space, and lie down for a nap. I wake up at a little after five, and step out onto the balcony to look at the city, hoping Mark is close. I want to have my driver take me to him, sneak him into the luggage compartment of the vehicle, and head straight to the airport from there. We don't know how much the enemy knows, and I have to assume that they've gotten into Gardner's files by now.

I'm grimacing at the smell of the polluted air, when the bullet tears into my guts. I never hear the shot. In an instant, I'm laying on the balcony floor, gritting my teeth against the pain. I check the wound out quick, and see that it is small caliber, entry only. Not a lot of blood. The slug is probably lodged somewhere in my digestive tract.

No chance of standing up, too much pain. I push myself back into the room with my feet, and grab my phone. I mean to send a quick text to Jack, but as I am fumbling the phone trying to get the code typed in to unlock it, the door bursts open. Three men. Big. Screaming at me.

They come to pick me up, and I chuck my phone out the window. The collision with the pavement seven stories down will destroy it. The phone will automatically send out an alert to Jack and a few other people at Reeder when it shatters.

As I watch the phone sail over the balcony railing, the three men unceremoniously yank me off the floor and haul me down the stairs to the parking garage where the black Suburban I rode in on sits idling. My driver lies next to it in a pool of blood, and I can see an exit wound from a small caliber round in the back of his head. They throw me inside, and one of them jumps in back with me while the other two get in front and start to drive. The one in back stuffs my face down into the seat. I think for a moment he means to suffocate me, and I turn my head so that I can breathe. He says something in Swahili, punches me in the right kidney, and stuffs my head down harder. He doesn't want to smother me; it wouldn't make sense for them to kill me now. They are taking me somewhere, and don't want me to see.

I've gone through training for this. Stay calm, assess everything, count turns, catalog sounds, stops, and speed. They take me in a few crude circles around the center of the city. We can't be more than a few blocks from the hotel, even though we've been driving for almost a half hour. They open the door and pull me out, and I see that we are in a large open building. It's either a warehouse or hangar, or some other similar type of place.

The three men drag me through a small door, and into what looks like an office. I am roughly thrown into a wooden chair with no padding on the seat or back. Across from me is another man in another wooden chair. He has blonde hair and is built with a lot of muscle, but beyond that I can't tell anything about how he looks. He's been beaten to such a pulp that his face is a mush of blood and missing teeth. His cheeks, lips, and the areas around his eyes are swollen completely out of shape. If he wasn't lolling his head around slightly now and then, I'd think he must be dead. His shirt is soaked red with blood, although the few places where it hasn't been drenched are canary yellow.

They tie me up, and before even asking any questions, they take turns whipping my thighs with an extension cord. They've cut

128

the plug end off of it, and the cord whistles as it arcs through the air. I know I am probably going to die here. They finally do start to ask questions in broken English, but instead of answer or even listen, I do what my training has taught me: Focus on something far away. Pieces of what they say come through here and there. "Who was assassin?" from one, then "How many men came to kill Unti?" from another. This goes on for about an hour. Apparently, I tire them out. All three sit on a couch on the far end of the room. More talk in Swahili.

The tallest, who also looks the youngest at about sixteen, walks across the room, smacking the back of my head when he passes by. He goes into a door that was slightly open when they dragged me in here. It is a bathroom with one small window above the toilet. I run through the other information I know about this place, and try to think of possible escape routes. I could go back to the car. I haven't seen any other doors, but maybe I could find a roof access. Between all this, I think about Mark, and hope he's gotten word from Reeder that I am in trouble, and he should just haul ass to the airport. That should have been the plan all along. I can't help second-guessing myself, thinking that I never should have come here. Mark is a big boy, he can surely get from any hiding spot to the airport without my help.

The light that comes from under the closed bathroom door shifts as the teenage boy inside moves. Then I see the light shift in an odd way and hear a slight thump. A few second later, blood spreads out from the bathroom under the door, and runs onto the carpet of the room I am in. The other two don't notice. I look over to the beaten man, who must be Gardner. He slowly moves his head up and down in a *yes* motion to tell me he sees it, too. Even though his face is so swollen I can't see his eyes, he can see out of them enough to know that the boy in the bathroom is dead.

There's a gunshot from outside, and I see the heads of both the men on the couch explode. I look to their left, and there's a hole in the wall. I look to the man across from me and say, "Gardner, it's Mark. He's going to get us out of here."

Gardner tries to speak, but even his tongue is swollen and bleeding. I can't understand anything he says. It's another five minutes before Mark quietly comes through the door that leads to the car. He kneels before me and smiles. He looks like a guy on vacation, wearing Bola shades propped up on his forehead, a Hawaiian shirt, and linen pants. "Hey, boss. Think you can walk?"

I smile back at him. "Yeah, I think so. I took one to the belly."

As he turns to untie Gardner, he says, "Yeah, I saw it. I was about a block away watching you. I'd been tailing these three for a while. I think they're the only guys Nu'undi has in town right now."

"Nu'undi... I know that name. He take over for Unti?"

"Help me with Gardi." I try to get under Gardner's left arm so that we can drag him, but standing up straight under his weight hurts my bullet wound too much.

"It'll tear me open if I stand up straight and flex, Mark." He nods, and simply throws Gardner over his shoulder in a fireman's carry.

As we are making our way to the car, me hobbling, Mark grunting in effort to carry Gardner, who I now see is not just well-muscled but sort of oxen-like, Mark grunts out, "Nu'undi is Unti's oldest son. He's in charge now. The good thing is that he's an idiot." We get Gardner into the back seat as gently as we can, but he still cries out in pain twice. Mark turns to me and smiles again, "Nu'undi thinks condoms are sent from the CIA to give him cancer. I watched him a lot while I was at the compound. He's got symptoms of HIV."

I nod, and we get in the car. Mark starts it, and I look over to him. "Mark, text Jack."

"Way ahead of you, boss. He's got the jet hot. Just in case Nu'undi has another team in town, we're taking the back way to the airport."

***

By the time we get off the jet after a short flight to an American Air Force base in Qatar, Mark is drenched with our blood. There are stains all over the aircraft. I'm patched up pretty good, but the best he could do for Gardner was so try and wrap his face in gauze. I walk down the steps behind Mark, where a doctor is waiting with a stretcher. He smiles at me, and says, "We've got a surgical room prepped for you." I nod, and let him help me onto the gurney. There's a second team waiting to get Gardner off the plane. Mark goes immediately to them. "I bandaged his face, but I think all of his fingers were broken. They burned his feet, too." That's the last thing I hear before the doc gives me a shot and the world goes black.

***

I'm out for about three days. Infection sets in, and I'm isolated for another two weeks. A flight to Germany for more recovery, lots of phone calls home to Kelly. Jack calls twice, but his Tango is now a Zulu and on a mission in Serbia. I mention that Serbia is pretty much right next door to Germany and Jack laughs off the insinuated invitation to visit. No hide nor hair of Mark.

By the time I get off the jet to meet Kelly at the hangar nearly three weeks after I left her for the mission, I'm convinced that my career is over. I hug her close, and whisper into her ear, "I think they're going to make me retire."

She kisses me hard and whispers back, "I sure as God hope so, Greg. I can't do it anymore."

We walk to the car hand-in-hand. On the way home we stop for ice cream and talk about how we met. My phone rings. I look at Kelly. "It's Mark."

She nods, looks a bit concerned, and says, "Take it." She's trying to be supportive, I know, but I can sense the edge in her voice the way nobody else can.

I answer. "Mark, buddy! I thought maybe you were a figment of my imagination there for a while. Where have you been?"

"Ha. Yeah. Uh…" This is totally unlike him, and my internal red flags start going up. "Greg, I'm really sorry I couldn't visit. I got reassigned."

"Reassigned?"

"Yeah. I can't talk about it. I just wanted to call and say thank you for everything. For training me, for coming to bail me out of Africa, for showing me the ropes. I wouldn't have my new gig without you."

"So what is this new gig? Cover Thirteen?"

131

"No, no. Nothing like that. This is one that I'm pretty sure you've never heard of. I really can't talk about it."

"Mark, I've got top clearance—"

"Greg, I'm sorry. I'm moved to a new place. This is the last call I can make to you, buddy."

"Wow. This must be some really high-end stuff. You sure it's what you want?"

"Yeah, yeah." He pauses. "Greg, thanks again. Once this assignment is up, I'll come visit."

"Okay. Sounds good, buddy. Bye."

"Good-bye, Greg."

I hang up the phone and look to Kelly. She's concerned. "Greg, what is it? You look pale."

"It's Mark. He's with another agency now."

"Doing what?"

"He can't tell me."

"Whoa. Must be big." She takes my hand. "Let's go home. I've got the bed made and candles laid out. I want to celebrate you coming home alive and well."

A week later, I sit at my office desk at Reeder, wondering what's going to happen to me now. There's a quiet knock on the door, and Jack pokes his head in. I smile. "Here to tell me I have to retire?"

He chuckles and smiles. "No. Here to give you a file on your next Tango. We can't go around kicking out our best Primes just because they got shot, can we?"

***

The next time I see Mark is in a photo in *Time* magazine. He's in the crowd behind some Secret Service goons. Mark is dressed like he's on vacation and standing in the middle of a crowd of onlookers, blending in perfectly, so I'm pretty sure he's on a job. In the foreground of the photo, a candidate for Senate from New York lies in a pool of blood.

I analyze the photo over and over. I find and read the file on the candidate. He had some issues with the mob, and the FBI believed he was a religious zealot. Nothing too out of sorts for a conservative New York politician, really. The file actually seems a bit thin, if anything.

The man arrested for the fatal shooting is the obvious choice, crazy as hell and known to tweet threats to politicians every few days. It all fits perfectly, but something doesn't sit right. I do some more digging on the candidate, and find a paper he wrote in grad school proposing that the best solution to the population overgrowth of the human race is to use neutron bombs against the most highly populated regions in Asia. I print the paper and add it to my copy of his file.

When I get home, Kelly smiles. "You got something in the mail that looks like a letter." She hands it to me. The envelope has my name and address handwritten. The return address is Langley. Nobody in the CIA writes letters. I open the envelope and see Mark's handwriting. It reads *BLACK VINE BLACK VINE BLACK VINE STOP READING.*

Black vine. It was our code for poisoning Unti's water supply. I look at the envelope again. No postmark.

I'm sitting on the side of my bed now, running through all these thoughts and writing them down as I remember them. Mark knows I am researching the job he was just on. He knows that I saw the photo. He is almost certainly telling me to stop looking into the death of the senate candidate or I'll be poisoned. I have to trust him. In the morning, I'm going to use a file destruction system in the office to burn my files on the candidate... Unless they've already hit my well with poison, in which case, I'll die in my bed with my wife.

www.ingramcontent.com/pod-product-compliance
Lightning Source LLC
Chambersburg PA
CBHW051844170626
46807CB00003B/1348